Via CRUCIS
Via LUCIS

A catalogue record for this
book is available from the
National Library of Australia

Via CRUCIS
Via LUCIS

The Way of the Cross
The Way of the Light

BROTHER BRAD SMITH

Dedication

To God be the glory
through our Lord Jesus Christ.

Dear reader, I pray that this publication will help
you to deepen your relationship with Jesus.

All praise to God, the Father of our Lord Jesus Christ.

*It is by his great mercy that we have been born again,
because God raised Jesus Christ from the dead.*

*Now we live with great expectation,
and we have a priceless inheritance—
an inheritance that is kept in heaven for you,
pure and undefiled, beyond the reach
of change and decay.*

1 Peter 1:3–4

Acknowledgements

As a teenager I was deeply moved by the assessment of the crucifixion in the book *Who Moved The Stone?* by Frank Morrison (OM Publishing, 1983). Until that point I had taken for granted that there wasn't any controversy around the events listed in the Biblical records concerning the timeline of the death of Jesus Christ.

Was there really any mixup in the recorded events by the different gospel authors, or could there be a simple and logical explanation that lays out the pattern of what happened in that eventful day in history? Whilst reading the book it became apparent that if we were to dig deeply into the Word of God then we should find answers that complement or help to interpret other passages of scripture.

As a young Christian, I was asked by more 'mature' Christians to take some things *by faith;* but to me that meant accepting what seemed to be inconsistencies within the written Word about some aspects of scripture. It didn't always make sense. As an adult, and working as engineer for some 30 years now, I needed to understand things from a logical perspective, and having had the opportunity to undertake research into the Gospel events, I have longed to capture them in a logical manner for others to follow. Hence my deep interest in developing this book.

I have also leaned on the journalistic efforts to sift through arguments surrounding the resurrection, presented in *The Case for Christ* by Lee Strobel (Zondervan Publishing, 1998) and have enjoyed many a long read of *Evidence that Demands a Verdict* by Josh McDowell (Zondervan Publishing, 2017). This is what I aim to present — via interpretation — in the *Via Crucis* section of this book.

The inspiration for the *Via Lucis* section of this publication has come from *Stations of the Light* by Mary Ford-Grabowski (Image Publishing, 2007). Without her depth of research and extensive analysis into the *Via Lucis*, I would have spent many months undertaking the research required to assemble this material.

Her work has enabled me to digest, meditate and reflect on the stations of the cross and the stations of the light. As you will be able to tell from my writing style, I like to bring the reader in to the scene that is developing through the pages of the Bible, and engage in the unfolding development in a way that helps to see through their eyes. This was made so simple for me to do through her writings, and also complemented my writing style immediately.

Inspiration from one of Mary's quotes struck a chord with me to write this book:

> *We are called to be crucifers and lucifers, cross bearers and light bearers, not literally like the ministers who carry the cross and light at the beginning of every liturgical procession, but symbolically as pilgrims who were given this vocation at baptism.*

(Ford-Grabowski: 2007, p21)

Contents

Introduction

It was early and I was praying quietly in bed, the day had not yet begun.

Easter 2022 had just passed, and during my prayer time I was reflecting on the 14 Stations of the Cross.

If you have participated in the 14 stations then you would understand that this holy ritual takes us through the last 24 hours of Jesus' life before his death: from praying in the Garden of Gethsemane to being laid in the tomb.

As a non-Catholic Christian, I had never been offered the opportunity to take part in the 14 Stations of the Cross, though I had seen and read about them in various churches that I had travelled to from time to time. Occasionally it would appear on television around Easter time, but it wasn't part of my everyday Christian experience or tradition.

This was something new and personal to me.

As I was praying that morning, I heard the Lord say to me, 'Brad, look into the 14 stations of the resurrection.' I didn't know if such a thing existed, as I had only been acquainted with the 14 stations of the cross. It didn't take long before I realised that this was a fairly new concept in the history of the church, and I became acquainted with Mary Ford-Grabowski's book *Stations of the Light*.

Her book explains the concept and historical challenges of the 'Traditional Stations of the Cross', which do not have a complete set of Biblical references. However she notably mentions that Pope Paul VI assembled the 'New Stations of the Cross' in 1975 with strictly Scripture based stations and offered them 'as an alternative to the faithful few'. (Ford-Grabowski:2007, p32)

Following along the same lines as the New Stations of the Cross, her book *Stations of the Light* presents fourteen stations that follow Jesus from the point of His resurrection to His ascension and pouring out of the Holy Spirit, using strictly Scripture based references. These are based on fourteen Biblical references, which were introduced as a Roman Catholic devotion at the end of the twentieth century, when the Vatican was preparing the Jubilee Year.

From these two sets of Biblical references we have a complete set of Stations — fourteen in each of the *Via Crucis* and *Via Lucis* — that walk us through the death, resurrection, ascension and ministry of Jesus Christ.

Inasmuch as I have desired to stay solely with Biblical references for all Stations, I felt the need to draw on extra-Biblical sources to provide some details where the Gospels were silent or information was absent. For instance, the names of the criminals who died on either side of Jesus are not printed in the Bible, however they are mentioned in apocryphal writings — albeit dependent on different traditions as to whether the names are this or that. For these reasons, this devotional has been classified as Biblical fiction.

Out of respect, I have presented the English word 'God' in the Jewish format 'G-d' in most places. Jewish cultural beliefs hold the name of God in such high esteem that they prefer to avoid saying or writing the Name in its entirety. Instead of feeling insulted or irritated by this writing style, could you please *attempt* to embrace the origins of Christian beliefs, and take a look through the eyes of Jewish culture in this regard?

I've also tried to correct some non-Biblical references that have inspired tradition from history or apocrypha. For instance the Bible never stated that the nature of the crime of the two that were crucified with Jesus, so I've kept strongly with the term 'criminal' to describe the reason for their crucifixion, rather than 'thief' which is the more widely accepted version that has been adopted by extra-Biblical sources. At best, the Biblical records confirm that they were involved in an uprising against the Roman empire, and therefore worthy of capital punishment.

My writing is not in any way intended to influence the reader away from the Biblical Word, but to provide a more personalised experience through which to view the fourteen Stations of the Cross and Stations of the Light.

I enjoy writing in the first person, known as pseudepigrapha (or pseudo-autobiography). To present the Stations through the eyes of each person I have undertaken many hours of research and reading through Biblical, extra-Biblical, apocryphal and historic sources; also taking into consideration viewpoints from authors in commentaries, and attempting to decode some conspiracy theories, but trying to avoid a *Dan Brown* style of authorship.

I want to take you on an adventure and help you to 'see through their eyes' at each of the 28 stations. I'm going to take you inside the mind of the disciples, of Peter, of Mary the Mother of Jesus, Mary Magdalene, Pilate, the soldiers, the Centurion, Thomas and others.

As you read and envelope yourself in the narrative, I want you to feel what they feel; to experience what is unfolding through their eyes; hear their heart beating in your chest; sense their disbelief, confusion, despair, amazement; and to question whether you would have felt the same way, if you had been there.

I hope you get it.

As a writer, I may sometimes take some liberality to convey a point; please don't judge me for this. Whilst my aim is to keep this as Biblically based as possible, I want you to experience a new dimension that you sometimes may not read from the pages of the written Word. I'm not trying to distort the Word of God — but rather, trying to bring the most out of it that I possibly can, so that you can enter more deeply into your relationship with Jesus Christ through the Stations of the Cross and the Stations of the Light.

The characters that you will encounter are people just like you and me; the Stations that they walk through are from the written and inspired Word of God (let's be clear — the Bible); and the events that they had opportunity to experience have been captured through the eyes of those who were there for us to see a glimpse of what was being experienced at the time.

If you're ready to join me and see through the eyes of those who lived through one of the most controversial times in the history of the human race, then let's start in the Garden with Jesus, and the few disciples with heavy eyes that He wanted to pray with, for what was about to take place: *the world's greatest story ever told.*

Brother Brad Smith

Via Crucis 1:

Jesus Prays

³⁹ Then, accompanied by the disciples, Jesus left the upstairs room and went as usual to the Mount of Olives.

⁴⁰ There he told them, 'Pray that you will not give in to temptation.'

⁴¹ He walked away, about a stone's throw, and knelt down and prayed,

⁴² 'Father, if you are willing, please take this cup of suffering away from me. Yet I want your will to be done, not mine.'

⁴³ Then an angel from heaven appeared and strengthened him.

⁴⁴ He prayed more fervently, and he was in such agony of spirit that his sweat fell to the ground like great drops of blood.

⁴⁵ At last he stood up again and returned to the disciples, only to find them asleep, exhausted from grief.

⁴⁶ 'Why are you sleeping?' he asked them. 'Get up and pray, so that you will not give in to temptation.'

Luke 22:39–42

⸺ *Tired* ⸺

John, the Beloved

We had just finished an emotional supper.

It wasn't our usual meal; we ate together as *the Twelve*, on one of the most celebrated nights of our indigenous calendar: *Pesach*, Passover, with our *Rabbi:* Jesus.

Historically it was a night of reflection and celebration, however it was cut apart with the Masters words, 'Here at this table, sitting among us as a friend, is the one who will betray Me.'

Each one, in turn, whispered to the one next to him, 'It's not you, is it?'

During the meal, at the dipping of the bread, I pressed in and asked, 'Is it me?'

Then moments later, the Lord handed the bread to the treasurer; their eyes locked across the table, and with just a few words, he left.

There was urgency in His voice, which left us confused. *What did we forget, on this night of remembrance?*

Fourteen centuries earlier, this very night was the exodus. We recalled the stories handed down to us by our fathers; and by their fathers; and by their fathers-fathers.

They had prepared for this night for many years; with great signs and wonders they saw what *the son of Pharoah's daughter Moshe,* Moses, had accomplished in the presence of the king. The Egyptian task masters kept them in slavery for 430 years, and demanded *'More! More!'* yet the work was never finished.

Their skin stretched tight and withered from the fiery sun scorched heat. The pain from a long day's work was unrelenting. They faced sleepless nights. And they were tired.

Yet Moshe refused to be called the son of Pharoah's daughter; the deliverer of Israel adopted his own people, rather than maintain the pleasures of Egypt.

Rebellion! Uprising! Revolt!

That's when *the time came;* that's when they fled their captors; that was the signal of their hope.

A candle flickered, bringing me back to the Olive Mount; we viewed the expanse of the city below and around from this lofty hilltop.

A quiet; a hush; *a silence.*

In this grove we stopped, and were asked to pray, just as we had many times; it was a favourite viewing spot of the kingdom. But tonight was of special concern. 'Pray that you do not give in to temptation,' He said.

Our thoughts jumped all over the word, *temptation.* The harder we thought, the more tiring it became.

Tempted for what?

That's confusing. I wasn't going to fall for it. I'm faithful to the end. Why pray?

Just five days earlier, we had come down this Mount. The Master had asked us to fetch a wild donkey — a colt — that had never been ridden, tied up outside the front door of a house in that nearby town.

Bringing the donkey to Jesus, garments were placed over it, and He sat down.

A crowd had gathered; such a spectacle hadn't been seen in Jerusalem. And yet, here a procession made way for the entry of a King.

The crowd parted up the laneway, and garments and leafy branches were spread out on the road ahead of Him.

Flanked on both sides, they shouted military welcome:

'Hosanna!
Blessings on the one who comes
  in the name of the Lord!
Blessings on the coming Kingdom
  of our ancestor David!
Praise G-d in the highest heaven!'

I was certain: This was the rebellion! This was the uprising! This was the revolt!

But what did it mean now, in this time of agony, at this rock where we were to pray?

The cool air lapped against our clothes in the light of the full lit moon, pressing us to stay awake. Falling to the ground, the night grew dim, and our eyes struggled to fight temptation for prayer, lest we rest.

He called the Three to pray with Him, just a stone's throw away: me, Peter, and James.

'Come.'

The word resonated within me, just as the first time He called me.

Come.

My mind raced.

My heart, pounding in my chest. My breath echoed heavily in the mist.

Here on this Mount *just two days ago* we heard of coming events, and persecutions, and terror that was to come.

Surely not, Lord?

Tonight, did this mark *the end of the age* that He disclosed?

> *There will be a great persecution.*
> *You will stand trial before kings and governors*
>   *on account of Me.*
> *You will be betrayed, even some will kill you.*
> *Everyone will hate you because of Me.'*

I wasn't ready for this, not *tonight.*

Not a betrayal.
Not a death.
Not on my watch.

There, by the rock, *the rock of anguish*, our Master
bled tears, with loud shouts and cries to the Almighty.

How could I sleep, along with these others, *with such noise?*

At that rock, we watched.
We waited.
And, unforgivably, *we slept.*

Suddenly, a giant glow split the night and it drew
back; heaven opened, and an angel appeared. The
agony of this earthly scene became disrupted by
the brilliance of the heavenly.

This was a *forever moment.*

'Strength. Strength. STRENGTH!'
came the angel's words.

Looking up, He prayed more fervently.

Until finally, the moment had come.

'Awake! Here comes my betrayer!'

Via Crucis

Via Crucis 2: Jesus Betrayed

45 *Then he came to the disciples and said,*
   Go ahead and sleep. Have your rest.
   But look — the time has come.

   The Son of Man is betrayed into the hands
   of sinners.

46 *Up, let's be going. Look, my betrayer is here!'*

47 *And even as Jesus said this, Judas, one of the twelve*
   disciples, arrived with a crowd of men armed with
   swords and clubs. They had been sent by the leading
   priests and elders of the people.

48 *The traitor, Judas, had given them a prearranged signal:*

   'You will know which one to arrest when I greet him
   with a kiss.'

49 *So Judas came straight to Jesus.*

   'Greetings, Rabbi!' he exclaimed and gave him the kiss.

Matthew 26:45–49

⸌The Kiss⸍

Judas, the Betrayer

I've been with Him — and the rest —
For three years now:
'Master', 'Rabbi', 'Teacher', 'Messiah'
That's what they called Him.

He says He is the Saviour of the World
And people love Him.
But I don't.
Well, *not any more*.

The miracles, the healings
He's just a people pleaser,
Self-absorbed
Bathing in the attention given.

The crowds
The crowds
Just keep getting bigger
Flocking to see Him act
To hear Him speak.

He's a rebel
Breaking down the structure of our society
His words cut through the law of our priests
And defy our age-old traditions.
Nothing but trouble.

And I grow envious
As I see His compassion and mercy
To heal the sick
To cast out demons
To receive this oil of a years' wages
And have it poured on His head
'To prepare for burial', He said
But the poor could use it.
Such waste
Such lack of respect
Such self-centredness.

And now my heart is stirred
Indignant.
This is the last supper
We celebrate our Passover in an upstairs room
Away from our families

And again, the Centre of Attention
Must counsel us
Must tell us how to live.
But not me.

It's over now.
I've resolved to be rid of Him
That His words
Shall no longer pierce my heart.
He won't rule over me
He's not my 'Lord'
At best, He's just a Rabbi, a Teacher.
Now in that room
Our eyes lock.
I want to look away, but can't.
We both reach for the bowl
We both dip our bread in the sauce
Together — and I've tried to avoid this —
We pause
Deadly silence
My heart is pounding
Here comes another lecture
Another condemning speech.
Just wait.

The Master stopped
And gazed around the dimly lit room
To the eleven others
Who were here to eat,

Here to remember,
Here to connect.

'Tonight,' and there was a long pause
'Tonight, one of you will betray Me.'

Shock.
Commotion.
Denial.
Then … *silence.*

'The one who dips his hand in the bowl with Me.'
Our eyes meet again:
Locked.
My heart burst with fury
Exposed, I felt guilt rise
Angry, I withdraw my hand
Gasping, I leaned back in my chair.

The Master had spoken
He knew,
He knew.
But also,
'What you need to do, do quickly.'
And I left
To the confusion of the Eleven.

Gasping, I ran outside to catch my breath
Those words, pierced again my heart.

So running, I found the priests
Gathered to discuss this Enemy
This Tyrant
This Anarchist
That people loved
Who berated and belittled their authority,
Who questioned their righteousness,
Who exposed their hearts and motives.
He had to go.
It was his time.

And I came to the meeting
As a friend, a supporter
To promote their cause
To sympathise with their ambition
To demonstrate my allegiance
As I'd promised them.

For silver thirty pieces
I would arrange a signal, a sign
Tonight.
Tonight in the Garden
That's where they will meet
And you can arrest Him there
With no crowds, no people.
Under a full lit moon.
Tonight.

'Agreed,' they roared
And passed me the money bag
As payment for my services
Fulfilling my role
To restore order and peace to Israel.

Urgency pounded my chest
My heart exploding with the mission
I knew where to take them
To the summit, the peak, the Garden
Where the Teacher took us
Many times before.

Now, set and ready
The flicker of a torch
Weapons on hand
The battle for order began
And we trudged towards
That grove of olives, near the rock.

'Behold, here comes My betrayer,'
The words echoed in the night
Above the clamber
And again, pierced my heart with guilt and fervency.

'Betrayer?'
I won't be preached at.
I won't have anyone look down at me
I've played my position in the group
I've done my job

I'm not a second-rate treasurer
And I'm not a tax collector.

Then seizing the time
I stepped forward
To seal the fate of the One
Whom I despised
Who stole my glory
The Teacher, who did no wrong
His time had come.
Now I was in control.
And He must die.

The kiss
The kiss
That was the sign.

No — not an embrace —
This isn't a reunion —
The territory is set
The Man is mine
And I've been paid.
My job is done.

And they led Him away.

All night it's been
Waiting
Waiting for decisions
Waiting for action

To rid this Man, this Rebel
From Israel.

And then
Agreed.
This Man to die,
Today
Confirmed.
Confirmed.

I did it
Yes, *I did it.*

Was that *relief?*
Was that *justice?*
Was that *indignation?*
Was that *pity?*
Was that *anger?*
Was that *self-condemnation?*

My mind racing.
My soul disturbed.
And panic.
Fear.
Abandoned.

No absolution
What have I done?
Am I going crazy?
I needed this, so badly.

The coins in my hand scream at me
Shouting, *'You condemned an innocent man'*
They sing in my mind, *'You murderer, you fool.'*
Accused.
Accused.
Guilty.
Remorse.

The law declares *'You shall not condemn an
    innocent man'*
And yet, righteous-am-I
These coins testify,
Testify.
Against me.
These coins,
These coins.

I must remove
The guilt of my shame
To cleanse my regret
And be rid of this testimony
To stop this insanity
I must return.

To the Temple
There they gather, warming around a fire
I need to offload.
'What's that to us?' they snarl,
Rejecting my confession.

There's no way
Forgiveness eludes me
The priests resolve to disown me
And I reject their coins —
Thirty pieces —
Sprayed back into the Temple
The home of the righteous
To end this testimony.

The *remorse*
The *grief*
The *betrayal*
The *testimony*
The *rejection*
The *absolution*
To end it all
To escape the insanity of my own mind.

Where did I go wrong?
Could this really be the end?
The Master must die today
And that was not their concern,
They put that on *my head*.

Heart pressured with resolve
Rejecting the Teachers words
Abandoned to let my heart rule
Denying the conviction —
Those piercing words —
Of Him they called their Saviour.

Would I do it again?
Should I be so concerned in my own plot
And in my own story
That I fail to heed the warnings
That I stop hearing the voice of the Master
That I allow the Dark Prince to speak to me?

If I had my time all over again
As one of the Twelve
Would I do it again?

Via Crucis 3:
Jesus Condemned

53 *They took Jesus to the high priest's home where the leading priests, the elders, and the teachers of religious law had gathered.*

54 *Meanwhile, Peter followed him at a distance and went right into the high priest's courtyard. There he sat with the guards, warming himself by the fire.*

55 *Inside, the leading priests and the entire high council were trying to find evidence against Jesus, so they could put him to death. But they couldn't find any.*

56 *Many false witnesses spoke against him, but they contradicted each other.*

57 *Finally, some men stood up and gave this false testimony:*

58 *'We heard him say,*

*'I will destroy this Temple made with human hands,
and in three days I will build another, made without
human hands.'"*

⁵⁹ *But even then they didn't get their stories straight!*

⁶⁰ *Then the high priest stood up before the others and
asked Jesus,*

"Well, aren't you going to answer these charges?

What do you have to say for yourself?"

⁶¹ *But Jesus was silent and made no reply.*

Then the high priest asked him,

"Are you the Messiah, the Son of the Blessed One?"

⁶² *Jesus said, "I am. And you will see the Son of Man
seated in the place of power at G-d's right hand
and coming on the clouds of heaven."*

⁶³ *Then the high priest tore his clothing to show his
horror and said, "Why do we need other witnesses?*

⁶⁴ *You have all heard his blasphemy. What is your verdict?"*

"Guilty!" they all cried. "He deserves to die!"

⁶⁵ *Then some of them began to spit at him, and they
blindfolded him and beat him with their fists.*

*"Prophesy to us," they jeered. And the guards slapped
him as they took him away.*

Mark 14:53–65

The Blasphemy

Caiaphas, the High Priest

They'd been going all night; the plan had hatched and they got their man. The wiry shadows formed echoes on the cold stone walls behind them, the light of the flames also keeping them warm.

They were tired, and edgy.

It started with a kiss, in the olive grove at the foot of the hill, by the traitor.

That was the sign, the go-ahead, for the handover. A dozen men, praying — or sleeping — keeping watch; history's next moments would be preserved forever.

The rabble moved in, claimed their man; bargaining for their freedom, the Man said, 'Let these others go.' A commotion, a sword struck an ear; the ear restored to proper function, and the others fled.

Bustling down the slope, the Man restrained, towards the house of the High Priest. It was nothing fancy, but most convenient —the first stop on the way to the Governor. We needed a verdict, *tonight*.

The court of the accused was set: construed of religious leaders, the pious, self-righteous and virtuous religious. No-one was to leave innocent today, the verdict was pre-established.

The trial began — one said this, one said that — 'The testimony of two are required' — but no two *agreed*. Finally, the chief stepped forward with the charge, 'Tell us, aren't you the Christ, the Son of G-d?'

Quiet. Eyes scanned the room.

A swooping hush fell on the crowd, waiting the reply.

The charge was one of serious blasphemy — the law forbade anyone to equate themselves with G-d — and the answer was the death penalty.

Eying his captors around the room, Jesus said, 'You have said it.' Angry snarls became cynical smiles.

The room erupted into an insidious infection of laughter, filled with spite and sweat, and spitting the ground, the high priest tore his clothes, crying out loud, 'Blasphemy! We don't need witnesses — we have a confession!'

'Worthy! Worthy! Worthy!' They chanted with painful glee, knowing the charge would stick.

> *As good as dead.*
> *The world be rid of him!*

This Christ, this *son of G-d*, is merely man.

> *He won't rule us — we won't let it.*
> *We earned our place here.*
> *This man is not come to take it from us.*
> *We will see to that!*

Blow by blow, they beat him.

Slap, slap, slap, they cursed him.

Spit flowed mockery, they demanded, "Who hit you, Christ?"

The council adjourned: 'Guilty!'

They led the accused Blasphemer, bound, to the Governor for execution.

Via Crucis 4:

Jesus Denied

54 *So they arrested him and led him to the high priest's home. And Peter followed at a distance.*

55 *The guards lit a fire in the middle of the courtyard and sat around it, and Peter joined them there.*

56 *A servant girl noticed him in the firelight and began staring at him.*

Finally she said, "This man was one of Jesus' followers!"

57 *But Peter denied it. "Woman," he said, "I don't even know him!"*

58 *After a while someone else looked at him and said, "You must be one of them!"*

"No, man, I'm not!" Peter retorted.

59 *About an hour later someone else insisted, "This must be one of them, because he is a Galilean, too."*

60 *But Peter said, "Man, I don't know what you are talking about."*

And immediately, while he was still speaking, the rooster crowed.

61 *At that moment the Lord turned and looked at Peter.*

Suddenly, the Lord's words flashed through Peter's mind:

"Before the rooster crows tomorrow morning, you will deny three times that you even know me."

62 *And Peter left the courtyard, weeping bitterly.*

Luke 22:54–62

⌒*My Denial*⌒

Peter, the Rock

He called me 'The Rock', and rightly so.

> I proved myself to Him so many times; I am
> firm in strength of soul and unquestionable
> in my reasoning. The others know that I
> am a born leader; like a sturdy mountain
> overlooking a city. I've earned this title, by
> the revelation that *G-d gave me,* and I intend to
> use it.

> To me, to me *personally,* did He hand the keys
> of the kingdom of heaven. I've been granted
> authority to bind things in heaven and loose
> things on earth by special command. This is
> the favour granted me.

I had spoken up, taken charge and *reprimanded* the Lord for His mistake. There is no way that I would let the Master die at the hands of the elders and leaders of Israel, even if He felt that way. I will make sure of it; it's my responsibility. My oath!

'Heaven forbid, Lord. This will never happen to you.'

There was a pause, a heavenly silence, and I wasn't prepared for the words that were to flow next.

'Get away from Me, Satan. You are seeing things merely from a human point of view, not from G-d's.'

I was shocked. Dumbfounded. Outraged.

And … guilty.

I had overstepped my boundary.

I resolved: *That won't happen again. I'll never leave Your side.*

Two of the Three had followed the procession to the courtyard from a distance, waiting and watching to see the outcome of this trial by night.

We knew them all by name — Annas, the father-in-law to the high priest; Caiaphas, the high priest himself who prophesied, 'It is better that one man die for the people;' and the rest; so we stood in the shadows.

The cool air sent shivers up my spine; the smoke from the fire pit begged me to get closer. So I edged forward.

Warming, watching, waiting.

I could hear the outrageous discussion from the courtyard below that upper room. Inside there was turmoil: one shouted this; another that. From my vantage point, no charges would stick. *He's off.*

Good.

I couldn't bear to think what would happen if they got Him killed.

A young girl passed me as she drew near the fire, a servant to Caiaphas. Her gaze made me uncomfortable. Was she staring? What did she want? Please, *turn away*.

'Hey, aren't you one of those with Jesus of Nazareth?'

I was gob-smacked.

My cover was undone, and I needed to escape.

Easier to deny this charge, than to create a scene.

'I don't know what you are talking about.' I left.

There, out near the door; I'll stand by the entry way. Then I can still hear what was going on upstairs, and defend my Lord when I need to.

In the distance a rooster crowed. It was just before sun-up.

Persistent, the servant girl continued, telling the others that were there, "This man is definitely one of them."

She was determined to keep me honest.

Exasperated, I couldn't help myself.

I needed to save my skin.

What would they do to me, if they knew I was with Jesus?

Was this some deadly game in operation?

What was their play?

I denied it again, 'Honestly, I don't know the man.'

Uncomfortable, I moved outside. My thoughts started to fragment; I was breaking out in a sweat; my body started to quiver and convulse under the pressure of the moment. As we huddled around the glowing embers we discussed what might happen next, and were overheard by yet others in the courtyard.

I was confronted again, this time by another.

'You must be one of them, because your accent gives you away. You are Galilean.'

My self-control disappeared; *fuming*.

I hated myself.

I fumbled a strong reply to keep up the act.

'A curse on me if I'm lying — I don't know this man you're talking about!'

Immediately, the rooster crowed again.

My words rang like bells in my ears.

And in that moment, my mind flashed back to the journey up the mount earlier this evening, before the arrest.

> The Master was adamant — we were useless to Him.
>
> Jesus' steady tone of voice grasped our attention. 'All of you will desert Me.'
>
> *Silence.*

I pressed in; I needed to make it clear that He called me the Rock; He can rely on me.

'No, Lord. Even if everyone else deserts You, I never will.'

Stopping on the path, His arm rested on my shoulder in a form of reassurance, before saying,

'Peter — I am telling you the truth — this very night, before the rooster crows twice, you will deny me three times.'

You've got it wrong.

You don't know me.

I've made my resolve, and I'm sticking with it. It's time that You need to understand. I will always be here for You, because *You know that I love You.* And I will express my love for You, even in death!

'No! Even if I have to die with you, I will never deny You!'

And all the others vowed the same.

No more words were said, and we continued up the mount, to the olive grove.

The wretched agony of truth.

Oh, what a helpless man I am!

Grief, pangs of grief, seized and overtook me.

My body buckled under the pain, the realisation,
that I had failed.

On the ground, eyes flooded with tears of
anguish, my soul burst. It could not be contained.

I could not think.

The weight buried me; I broke down, and wept.

Via Crucis 5:
Jesus Judged

20 *Pilate argued with them, because he wanted to release Jesus.*

21 *But they kept shouting, "Crucify him! Crucify him!"*

22 *For the third time he demanded, "Why? What crime has he committed? I have found no reason to sentence him to death. So I will have him flogged, and then I will release him."*

23 *But the mob shouted louder and louder, demanding that Jesus be crucified, and their voices prevailed.*

24 *So Pilate sentenced Jesus to die as they demanded.*

25 *As they had requested, he released Barabbas, the man in prison for insurrection and murder. But he turned Jesus over to them to do as they wished.*

Luke 23:20–25

⁓The Decision⁓

Pilate, the Governor

Outside, the rabble were getting started.

Unbelievable. Couldn't they have chosen another day for this?

I could hear their commotion from before the crown of dawn; voices raised in the streets.

Was this going to be another uprising?

This was not a normal day — for them — it marked the historic sacrifice of a lamb that *apparently* freed them from the clutches of their Egyptian rulers.

> Legend has it, that on this night, a destroying angel killed all the sons of Egypt's first born; from the first born of the king, to the first born of the slave woman. Even the cattle in

the field lost their first born, such was the tragedy. And yet, those who painted the blood of the lamb above their door posts were miraculously delivered. They escaped their captors, and walked to freedom with their arms full of silver and gold; all the while leaving a nation in wailing behind them.

Tonight, there was something eerie in the air that I simply couldn't ignore.

Of all the days in the Roman calendar, today marked a time when I entertained the wishes of the religious class, those who ruled *the unruly*, with the laws that came from their priesthood. Over the years it became my custom to mimic their Passover, and release a prisoner as a sign, a symbol, of my rulership over them.

I held a delicate balance — commissioned with the power of Rome to execute law and justice at my command; and holding the sway of power over the disparate people that make up the land.

This rabble was becoming uneasy.

No, not just uneasy, they were getting riotous.

And that put me on edge.

Were they starting their own rebellion?

Outside my doors, a brood of snarling, grimacing priests demanded an audience. They refused to come in to meet me, because in their view, *I was unclean,* and they didn't want to defile themselves for their ceremony by entering my presence.

Here we go again.

I confronted the angry mob, 'What do you want?'

They pressed the Man before me, hands tightly bound. Clearly, a prisoner needed attention.

They began to state their case: 'This man has been leading our people astray by telling them not to pay their taxes to the Roman government and by claiming that he is the Messiah, a king.'

Hmmm, a rebel? Let's sort this out quickly and quiet the rabble.

I went out to the crowd and asked, 'What is your charge against this man?'

> 'We wouldn't have handed him over to you if he weren't a criminal!'

> 'Then take him away and judge him by your own law,' I replied.

> 'Only the Romans are permitted to execute someone,' the Jewish leaders replied.

I went back into the quarters and called for Jesus.

'Are you the king of the Jews?'

I wasn't sure of the answer that I was expecting.

Jesus replied, 'Is this your own question, or did others tell you about me?'

'Am I a Jew?' I demanded. I knew little of their law — and didn't want to know.

> 'Your own people and their leading priests
>   brought you to me for trial.
> Why?
> What have you done?'

Jesus answered, 'My Kingdom is not an earthly kingdom. If it were, my followers would fight to keep me from being handed over to the Jewish leaders. But my Kingdom is not of this world.'

'So you are a king, then?'

Jesus responded, 'Yes, you say I am a king. Actually, I was born and came into the world to testify to the truth. All who love the truth recognize that what I say is true.'

My mind raced — who speaks like this? *What is truth?*

The priests ruckus continued, slinging accusations that wouldn't stick. Simply, this Man claimed to be a king. *What was that to me?*

The chief priests all stood outside my door, and became insistent,

'He is causing riots by his teaching wherever he goes — all over Judea, from Galilee to Jerusalem!'

'Oh, is he a Galilean?'

When they confirmed this, I sent him to Herod Antipas, who happened to be in Jerusalem at the time. Galilee was under Herod's jurisdiction, and Herod was delighted at this rare opportunity to see Jesus, because he had heard about him, and had been hoping for a long time to see him perform a miracle. He asked Jesus question after question, but Jesus refused to answer.

Meanwhile, the leading priests and the teachers of religious law stood there shouting their accusations. Then Herod and his soldiers began mocking and ridiculing Jesus.

Finally, they put a royal purple robe on him and sent him back to me.

Although I was an enemy towards Herod, *we became friends that day.*

I brought the chief priests together, the day was getting on. I wanted this dealt with before too much longer. It was already the second watch of the day, and there was nothing stopping me from freeing the Man.

'Listen, you rabble.
Both me and Herod found nothing that would call for the death penalty.
So we will have Him flogged and then release Him. There's nothing more we need to do.'

The religious elite demanded more. Accusations against Him *demanded* He die.

Jesus remained silent.

I needed to challenge Him further. 'Don't you hear all these charges they are bringing against you?'

But Jesus made no response, to my surprise.

The uproar was escalating.
My leadership was being questioned.
Was I fully executing my role under Rome's authority?

It was coming time for a decision, and it needed to be swift. So I addressed the crowd from my auspicious balcony, amidst the commotion of hundreds of people below.

'It is my custom, at this time of year, to release a prisoner during your feast.

I present to you:

> Barabbas — who you know as a murderer, and inciting insurrection against the government;

> And Jesus — who you call
> "The Anointed One".'

Slightly confused, this gave the crowd time to think.

Then I moved into position on the Judgement Seat, and waited for their response.

A messenger entered the room with a message from my wife that put my hair on end, saying:

> 'Leave that innocent man alone. I suffered through a terrible nightmare about Him last night.'

What omen was this?

It was time for a decision.

There was a lot at stake now, and time was getting away from me.

The priests were doing their thing, and the crowd started rioting.

The Prisoner was innocent, at least in my
eyes, of any wrong doing.

The exchange seemed fair, as it was out of
envy that they arrested Jesus.

My wife desperately begged me not to be
swayed by the religious elite.

And yet, here I am the appointed Governor,
hesitant to make the call.

I cried out again, 'Which of these two do you
want me to release to you?'

Barabbas!
BARABBAS!
BAR-ABB-AS!

Their song echoed a deathly melody
throughout the auditorium.

'Then what shall I do with Jesus, who is called the
Anointed One?'

Crucify!
CRUCIFY!
CRU-CI-FY!

A mixed chorus rose up from the crowd.

'But why? What crime has He committed?'

A mighty roar rose from the crowd.

I could see this was getting me nowhere.

They kept shouting, 'Crucify him! Crucify him! Release Barabbas!'

I was getting frustrated. They refused to listen to me, to the voice of reason, to my verdict of 'innocence'. They had a one-track mind, and I was agitated.

Clearly, this was an innocent man.
Clearly, they had another agenda.

If I was to go through with this, they couldn't pin it on me.

Emotionally spent, I cried out, 'But why? What crime has he committed? I have found no reason for the death sentence. So I will have Him flogged, and then I will release Him.'

But they insisted.

The atmosphere grew electric with blood curdling screams and taunts. The mob shouted louder, and more frenzied, demanding that Jesus be crucified.

They insisted that the Life be given to them. And it was mine to decide.

"BRING ME A BOWL!"

I was now angry. Quite angry.

> *How dare they manipulate my power and decision making?*

> *This mob knows nothing of authority.*

I washed my hands, and declared out loud to the crowd:

> 'I AM INNOCENT OF THIS
> MAN'S BLOOD!'

Let that be the end of the matter.

But they retorted, 'Let His blood be on us, and on our children!'

And with that, the decision was made.

Nodding to my private guard, I whispered faintly with a deep gulp, 'He's yours.'

Via Crucis

Via Crucis 6:
Jesus Scourged

1   *Then Pilate had Jesus flogged with a lead-tipped whip.*

2   *The soldiers wove a crown of thorns and put it on his head, and they put a purple robe on him.*

3   *"Hail! King of the Jews!" they mocked, as they slapped him across the face.*

John 19:1–3

⁓*The Scourge*⁓

Roman Soldier, Pilate's Guard

The morning sun was breaking through the open windows of the building, we were given a job to do. I ordered my regiment to the task.

'SOLDIERS — ON YOUR FEET!'

Their response was immediate; and they were ready for action. They longed for times like this. Rarely had they been given approval to carry out a *scourge;* they usually took it on themselves to treat the public away from the view of the commanding officers.

But this time was different.

This time, they could put their full weight behind it, *without shame.*

I stood at the entrance of the courtyard, a large open area we called the Quarters, where my men gathered for duty each day. The Quarters marked the start of the death sentence. In the centre, a tall pole stood upright, with bronze hook shackles above.

The Prisoner was brought in, and a circle formed.

The stench of earthy sweat, and gnarlish laughter garnished the mouths of my squad. Each would have the chance to take their turn in the proceedings.

'BEGIN!'

The game commenced.

It was a complete mockery of the scene that had unfolded before the Governor, just minutes earlier. And what would I care? This was mere *entertainment;* we don't often get the chance to hail a king!

'BRING ME THE KING!'

Two soldiers muscled up to the door, with the Prisoner in the centre. I wrenched the outer raiment from Him, top to toe, leaving Him exposed. My two helped to strip off the rest of the cloths, including a woven undergarment, wrestling Him to the ground, and stripped him bare. The clothes were thrown into a corner.

The squad roared, this was the beginning of the humiliation. We all pressed in to ridicule this poor bare condemned man; our stares formed a circle of intimidation.

'BRING ME A ROBE FOR THE KING!'

The soldiers scratched around the Quarters, and found a scarlet robe, worn by my men, and fixed it around his neck, loosely covering His nakedness. Kings wear royal purple robes, but in all mockery we only had this part of the upper uniform, so that is what we used.

'BRING ME A CROWN FOR THE KING!'

Venturing outside, they brought in a thicket of thorns, and wove it round. The spikes were as long as the palm of my hand, splendidly wrapped to form a crown. I was impressed with the glorious image that it would portray.

'PUT IT ON HIS HEAD!'

Holding Him in place, they grasped the razer-like crown, and pressed it down firmly into his skull. Immediately, thin, light blood pumped down the robe, over His body, spilling onto the ground.

The scene was fitting, but it lacked one thing.

'BRING ME A SCEPTRE FOR THE KING!'

A reed stick was brought in, nothing stately, and they fixed it into His hand. Propping the Slave into place against the pole, the men dropped to the ground in mock worship.

They spit upon Him, taunting Him with the words, 'Hail, King of the Jews!'

They used the reed to strike the thorns deeper, over and over, creating a persistent drenching of scarlet blood-red flow. It was time for the final act, one of softening up the body for the kill. *They don't try to escape after this.*

'BRING ME THE LEAD-TIPPED WHIP!'

It's as if the party had just begun; an outrageous cry rang out from the squad, who were preparing the thongs and ties. The Prisoner was ushered into the centre, and strapped to the pole.

Hanging there glibly, we commenced the work.

'ONE'

A harsh swack of lead and leather landed on the Victims back. The response was immediate, and comely.

The scream of the Victim was offset by joyous curdles from my men.

> The flagellum was a small hand-held whip; built with three separate leather strands and with small lead balls spliced throughout the strands. To keep the balls separate, and hence inflict as much pain as possible, the strands were slightly shorter than each other. This meant that they never landed near each other on the flesh that they consumed during the ordeal.

'TWO'

Another whack, across the back, exposed the bones beneath the skin. The jeers from the squad edged us on.

'THREE'

Searing intense pain. The Body writhed in agony, slithering around the base of the pole, then stopped, gasping for air.

'NEXT!'

Each man had his turn and so the scourging continued for some time. By the end, the Man's back was a bloodied mess of shredded flesh.

'AND NEXT!'

This time, no movement.

The whip had no effect.

'AND … ENOUGH'

The spectacle stopped when there was no response to the scourging that was being given.

Time was up.

The Body was useless to us now.

It was time to complete the next step in this killing.

Stripping Him of the *royal garments*, his own clothes were put back on Him.

And we led the King away to be crucified.

Via Crucis

Via Crucis 7:
Jesus Carries

[17]   *Carrying the cross by himself, he went to the place called Place of the Skull (in Hebrew, Golgotha).*

John 19:17

⁓*Alone*⁓

Jesus, the Only Begotten

Weighing heavily, My body drenched in blood
from head to foot.

The whipping had taken away My breath and My
strength; the bones in My back exposed to the
cool air.

The Roman guards' taunts and humiliations had
no effect; I was emotionally numb.

In that small moment of time where they let Me
be, My thoughts drifted to recount the past thirty-
three years of life.

'MOVE!'

The march towards Calvary began with a soldier
lifting me to my feet, and pointing down the hill.

'NOW!'

Looking into the distance, gathering the rest of my strength, I shuffled in the direction of the finger. And recalled the stories…

My mother cherished the memories, and often recounted them to Me, and the family.

> We were called to Joseph's town for the census, though I was heavily pregnant — so we made our way there on a small donkey. It took longer than expected as we had to tread carefully along the path. When we finally made it to Bethlehem, there was nowhere to stay.
>
> We came to his family, looking for a roof to cover our heads, some shelter from the journey we had endured — an aunt, an uncle, or cousins — but they wanted nothing to do with this Child; and besides, they were already hosting others who had moved into town for the roll call.
>
> Eventually, we found a place just outside town. It was no-one we knew, just a compassionate soul who saw our plight.
>
> It wasn't built for human accommodation; but a place where no-one could argue with us about the Child we bore.

To keep warm, we moved cattle out of the way and lay in their spot on the ground, under the rocky shelter that housed the other animals.

And that's where You were born — right there in the hay.

Yes, it was messy, and the straw was unfriendly to a new-born's skin.
And it was a most unpleasant and indignant way to enter the world.
But in that moment, we knew that we held a promise from G-d, the salvation of the world.

The memory came flooding back, full of emotion, just as my mother had recited it.

But in that moment, we knew that we held a promise from G-d, the salvation of the world.

'MOVE!'

Everyone knew that Joseph was not My real father. My mother was very young at the time, and she was pledged to marry Joseph at the time when she would be ready to have children. But before they could marry, while she was still pledged, an angel had visited her and described the blessing that would come her way.

It wasn't just *any* angel, it was the angel Gabriel, who stands in the presence of G-d Almighty.

'Don't be afraid, Mary,' the angel told her,
'for you have found favour with G-d!
You will conceive and give birth to a son,
    and you will name Him Jesus.
He will be very great and will be called
    the Son of the Most High.
The Lord G-d will give Him the throne
    of His ancestor David.
And He will reign over Israel forever;
    His Kingdom will never end!'

'But how can this be?' she asked, 'since I am a virgin.'

'The Holy Spirit of G-d and the power of the Most High will do this.

Your baby will be holy unto G-d,

And He will be called the Son of G-d.'

Mary responded, 'I am the servant of the Lord. May everything you have said about me come true.'

My mother's emotional words came flooding back. Everything that led up to this point has been driving me toward this one purpose: *to lay my life down for others, to restore the way back to G-d.*

Looking down at this dusty foot-beaten path, through drops of sweaty blood that continued down My clothes and mashed-up body, I placed one foot after another.

All realm of creation stared on — those nearby, others from roof tops; such a spectacle.

Earth and heaven hushed at the ensuing events.

Time paused, and waited.
Eternity stopped.

> *Ssssstep.*
> *Drrrrag.*
> *Swaaay.*
> *Balance.*
> *Wait.*
> *Breathe.*
> *Sigh.*

The weight of the prickly timber cross beam scorched into My exposed flesh, making this walk exhausting. My energy was drained from the scourge, not sure if I could complete this task, this walk of shame and humiliation.

In Jerusalem — the city of peace — many
untimely deaths of those who dared to come
against Rome.

Looking up — there — in the distance —
   a cursed mound.
'The Skull', they called it.

This fatal hill overlooked a valley.
And this would be My stopping place.

This is where the fight between good and evil
   would end.
At this hour, close at hand, would be the
fulfillment of all things, the end of the
Old Promises.

I'd given up My power, My status, My rights.
And here, subject to the Governor's
command, embraced a criminal's death.

Oh Jerusalem, why do you kill the prophets
and those sent to you?
How I wish today that you of all people
would understand the way to peace.
But now it is too late, and peace is hidden
from your eyes.

Determined, I broached another step.
Alone.

Via Crucis

Via Crucis 8:
Jesus Helped

21 *A passer-by named Simon, who was from Cyrene,*
was coming in from the countryside just then,
and the soldiers forced him to carry Jesus' cross.

Mark 15:21

⌒*The Chance*⌒

Simon, from Cyrene

Upon reflection, it was ten years ago *on this day* that changed my life.

I've always wondered, *Was it just a chance encounter, or did Yahweh have something planned for me that I was no yet aware of?*

My journey started eight weeks previous; it was my turn to represent our family unit at the annual *Pesach* celebration held in Jerusalem. Each year our clans would take turns as pilgrims to make the journey, and partake in the rituals, from each of our five families that lived there, and that year it was my role to make atonement for our family groups.

This time I took the pilgrimage with my two boys — Rufus and Alexander. In earlier times they were not quite old enough to travel, but this time they were strong enough for the trip and I wanted them to feel first-hand how their Jewish roots were lived out in practise. The effect of this would be fully captured at the *Passover* event in Jerusalem.

We were to travel by ship from Cyrene to Caesarea and then by foot to Jerusalem, and I had planned many father-son activities to do along the way. The trip would give us enough time together for me to explain our heritage, the stories of the patriarchs, entering the promised land, and how we ended up living outside the borders of Israel where we are now.

We lived in an area off the north coast of Africa, west of Egypt, that was settled as a Roman colony around two hundred years prior to our arrival. Our city was secure and the developed world was expanding along the coastline towns where Rome had access to rule. We had freedom so long as we got along with the ruling class of the day.

The trip in from the country was familiar to us; we travelled together with other families from our town who shared the faith of our father Abraham. The days were clear, and the nights were fresh. Neither too cold, nor too hot, to be unpleasant.

I planned to purchase the required offerings for the sacrifices once there; and for me this was a joyous event. We didn't do this every year, and at some point in the future I looked forward to being led by my sons on the same trip, where they would take up this responsibility for our family clans.

Now *that day,* we had slept overnight just outside the city in a small town, as we heard that there were limited rooms available. It was to be less than a Sabbath's walk to the altar, to ensure we could keep the piety that was expected by our leaders.

Arising early, we paid our dues to the inn keeper and tallied up what we needed for the day. Although we brought the Greek drachma, this needed to be changed to an acceptable offering for the temple. The price for the offerings was counted out — we needed enough to atone for our large family — and this required a certain number of sheep, goats and doves. I also put in extra coin, as I'd heard that the temple money changers were asking for more than the usual rate of exchange.

Approaching the city on the holiest day of our calendar meant that many people would be eager to make their way to the temple mount, and there would be a line to follow. Indeed, when we arrived there were many people lining the streets, the early morning rush reflected my past experience.

But there was more — not the solemn hush of the event; the city was in an uproar.

What was going on?

It was early morning, and one person was shouting after another; I'd not seen activity like this. The crowd was ecstatic, whipped into a frenzy, without decorum.

Like a swollen creek after heavy rain, a procession of soldiers cleared a path down the slope of the Via Dolorosa — pushing and beating people out of the way, leading the Prisoner to Golgotha, a few hundred metres down the hill.

We couldn't get through, so we stopped and waited and watched. There was no way we could miss this monumental event. I pressed the boys back into the sidewalls, and waited for the surge of soldiers to make way in front of us.

The Prisoner carried his cross, which was bearing heavy on his body; he carried the weight of the world with every step. Eventually, the scene unfolded within full view — we were within a body's length of the Victim.

Ssssstep.
Drrrrag.
Swaaay.
Balance.
Wait.
Breathe.
Sigh.

He stopped.

Wait, no, he slipped, and fell to the ground; His face smashing into the pavement.

Was this to be the end of the procession?

Angrily, a soldier stepped forward, and beat the Man. 'GET UP!'

There was no movement.

'GET UP!'

Again, the Body lay still on the ground: a bloody beaten mass of flesh lay before me, pinned by the beam.

The soldier was annoyed, and eyeing the crowd, he singled me out.

'HEY YOU!'

I looked away.
My eyes glanced side to side to see who was
    next to me.
There was no-one.
His eyes pierced my being.
I found it hard to swallow.
I didn't come here to be bound in this mess.
I'm just an onlooker, from out of town.
There was no escape.

'YOU! COME HERE!'

I stepped out, the soldier grasped my arm,
wrenching me into the open space in front of the
crowd, and the gasping Mess in front of me.

'NOW — CARRY THAT CROSS!'

I wasn't prepared for that, but I knew that if
I didn't immediately start to take action then I
could face the same fate as that wretched Soul.

Leaning forward, over the body, I lifted up the
blood-stained beam from off His shoulders,
prising it from His back. The sound of ripping
flesh tore through my ears as I tried to remove it
above His body; oozing blood had dried the cross
to His shoulders. Somehow, I got it separated.

'NOW — WALK!'

Suddenly, I was no longer a helper.
I was the centre of attention.
And I was being summonsed to take the walk
  to the end of the road, to the crucifixion site.

Looking up and forward, the crowd parted, and
the road revealed the destiny of those who had
walked a similar fate. Those were steps that I had
never intended to travel.

I looked back towards my boys, and with a nod
reassured them that I would return. The look in
their eyes told me a different story; they feared
that I would be next.

What had I gotten us into?

'MOVE!'

This soldier was not there to play games.
He needed to complete this job, clear the crowd
and finish off the Prisoner.

Settling the beam on my own back, and standing
upright, I moved forward, all the while keeping
watch over my shoulder on the soldier who was
shouting the orders.

From the corner of my eye I could see movement, the soldier erecting the Condemned onto His feet to complete the mission.

It was time for me to move.

But I couldn't help but ask, 'Why me?'

Via Crucis

Via Crucis 9:

Jesus and the Women of Jerusalem

27 *A large crowd trailed behind, including many grief-stricken women.*

28 *But Jesus turned and said to them, 'Daughters of Jerusalem, don't weep for me, but weep for yourselves and for your children.*

29 *For the days are coming when they will say, 'Fortunate indeed are the women who are childless, the wombs that have not borne a child and the breasts that have never nursed.'*

30 *People will beg the mountains, 'Fall on us,' and plead with the hills, 'Bury us.'*

31 *For if these things are done when the tree is green, what will happen when it is dry?'*

Luke 23:27–31

The Grief

Jesus, Man of Sorrows

Crushed, I lay on the ground listening to the wailing on the path behind me. Through their tears and sobs and heavy breathing, they echoed disbelief and dismay at the unfolding tragedy, whispering among themselves.

'Is He moving? Can He get up? Is He dead?'

Their loud screams and cries lamented my impending doom.

My senses were intact, even if My legs had fallen through. Though my vision blurred, the sound of Roman voices shouting or the lips of the women of Jerusalem whispering never stopped penetrating my ears.

In this moment, grief and sorrow came spiralling in, and I was overcome.

> I was not unfamiliar with it; my community never accepted me. I was teased to be 'Joseph's son' knowing that My mother was unwed at the time; so I grew up having been despised and rejected, and was acquainted with the deepest grief and hurt from my family's community.

> But this grieving was different; they needn't wail over my death.

> These women — although deeply touched, and were moved with the deepest of pain and anguish for the torment that I was experiencing — these women were to go through worse things than me. They did not know what was to come in 5, 10 or 20 years from now, how society would turn on them and tear their families apart. They didn't understand that my life was only temporary, and that my death would bring about eternal life.

> Didn't they read the prophet, the one who wrote about Me: *'I have set my face like a stone, determined to do His will'*? I have set my face like flint toward Jerusalem, and I am resolute in this task. Therefore, don't grieve for Me.

Turning to the women, I gasped a lament; each
exhausting breath taking all my strength.

> 'Daughters of Jerusalem,
>   don't weep for Me,
> but weep for yourselves
>   and for your children.

> For the days are coming
>   when they will say,

> 'Fortunate indeed
> are the women
>   who are childless,
> the wombs
>   that have not borne a child
> and the breasts
>   that have never nursed.'

I had already experienced a lifetime
   of grief and loss.
I had already laid My life down, *many, many times.*

But now, in this moment, I saw they needed
comfort for what was to come. They needed to
be able to draw strength and resilience to get
through the tough times in their lives.

And that is what I offered.

Grieve not for Me, daughters of Jerusalem, I have dealt with My own pain. Out of My suffering, My agony, and My death, I am offering you the strength to get through your own trials and difficulties. You do not have to deal with the grief of Me.

Via Crucis

Via Crucis 10:
Jesus Crucified

³² *Two others, both criminals, were led out to be executed with him.*

³³ *When they came to a place called The Skull, they nailed him to the cross.*

And the criminals were also crucified – one on his right and one on his left.

³⁴ *Jesus said,*

> *'Father,*
> *forgive them,*
> *for they don't know what they are doing.'*

Luke 23:32–34a

⏤*Final Words*⏤

Gestas, the Impenitent Criminal

BANG!
BANG!
BANG!

The hammer thrust down heavily onto the nail, piercing the wrist of my outstretched arm.

Pain thrashed inside me, finding its way up through my shoulder and neck, exploding in my veins and exiting through the base of my skull. I was being ripped apart from the inside, and my hand could not move.

'OTHER SIDE!' came the cry from the Centurion.

Again.

BANG!
BANG!
BANG!

This time my left wrist was fastened to the beam, my arms stretched wide.

Unable to move, I turned to see the Criminal forced on his back and lying on the beam next to me.

Fate was closing in.

'NEXT!'

They wasted no time in the process; the soldiers had consumed most of the entertainment the last hour at the Quarters, watching and abetting the procession down the slope.

'GIVE ME HIS HAND!'

The Criminal lacked the fight and energy to resist, whilst the soldiers wrung the wretched wrist into place.

BANG!
BANG!
BANG!

The sound echoed, the crowd watched, the leaders jeered and scoffed.

BANG!
BANG!
BANG!

And the left wrist was complete.

'LAST ONE!'

Quickly, they processed the last of us onto the timber slabs that would be used as our exposed coffin, where the world watched on.

I couldn't help myself — this didn't seem fair.

This Man, *this so-called Criminal,* was a Mage.

I'd seen him in action: healing the sick, casting out demons, performing signs and wonders among us. And that *not just once,* but for three years.

And yet, here he was, dying a criminal's death, unwilling to move.

He was *the hero of the people,* and right now, he could save us.

We didn't need to be here, strung out to die.

The way out of this was clear — *he just needed to act!*

> *Hey!*
> *Heeey!*
> *HEY!*

Do something.
Save us!
You saved others - save yourself!

Bah.
He would never listen to me.
I'm just a thief that got caught, with no way out.

My thoughts never escaped my mouth.

At that point, three burly soldiers were called to set me in position — one hugged me from my waist to lift my body upright; and one soldier hoisted each side of the cross beam, lifting it into position above their heads.

JOLT!

The battered human-timber assembly fell into place on the stationary stake, to form the shape of a cross.

The weight of my body stretched and elongated my arms by a hand-breadth; breathing became difficult.

My legs hung limply, but were soon snatched up and fixed to the pole with another large nail, forced into place with unforgiving brutality.

BANG!
BANG!
BANG!

Death was sure to be slow, and painful.

The Centurion painted on the charge board: CRIMINAL, and hung it on the cross above my head. All onlookers were warned that this was the penalty for my actions, a criminal deterrent.

On my right, the soldiers proceeded to process the other Criminal.

Same as me, they stretched out his arms, one by one, and fixed them into position on the cross beam.

And again, *JOLT!*

And followed by systemic hammering of the foot pin to fix the body into place.

In the background, they processed the last of us, hung aright for all to see.

The Governor had the charge written against the central Criminal in three languages: Hebrew, Aramaic and Greek.

It read: 'JESUS KING OF THE JEWS'

ישוע מלך היהודים

ܒܥܕ ܢܝ ܐܬ ܟܠܟ ܕܝܗܘܕܬܐ

ΙΗΣΟΥΣ ΒΑΣΙΛΙΑΣ ΤΩΝ ΕΒΡΑΙΩΝ

In Hebrew, the charge formed the acronym
YHWH. *Yahweh!*

> The Jewish leaders were angry and scoffed,
> demanding Pilate to change the sign to 'He
> said that he was the king of the Jews.' This
> would at least remove the incidental meaning.

> 'What I have written, I have written' was
> Pilates response.

Time lapsed.

My senses started to dull, but my heart resisted
— *we had the king of the Jews right here, and he refused
to help.*

We could escape the grip of death with a simple
command from 'the king'.

I was adamant that we needn't perish, and we
could be saved.

We just needed a saviour, a rescuer, to lead the revolt.

We didn't need to tolerate this barbaric Roman rule any longer — we have our own king, right here, next to us.

> *Jesus.*
> *Jesus.*
> *Don't you hear our pain?*
> *Don't you care we perish?*
> *If you're really the king of the Jews,*
>   *then save yourself!*

Faintly, the Criminal's head lifted to speak.

> *Maybe he heard my cries?*
> *Maybe this was the time when he could call on a legion*
>   *of angels and be rescued — taking us with him?*

My resentment was boiling over, though I was helpless to put anything into effect.

I was going to die here, *and he doesn't care!*

Faintly — but audible — from the King:

> *Father.*
> *FATHER.*
>
> *Forgive them.*
>
> *They know not.*
> *What they do.*

Exasperated, my miserable soul screamed hateful abuse — an involuntary reaction — all my thoughts released like a gushing stream.

At this time, in this hour of need, *forgiveness doesn't release the prisoner.*

This Man, this Criminal, this *King of the Jews* — surely, *he doesn't know the way to life, he can't help himself, let alone us.*

Via Crucis

Via Crucis 11:

Jesus and the Good Thief

³⁹ *One of the criminals hanging beside him scoffed,*
'So you're the Messiah, are you?
Prove it by saving yourself – and us, too, while you're
at it!'

⁴⁰ *But the other criminal protested,*
'Don't you fear G-d even when you have been
sentenced to die?

⁴¹ *We deserve to die for our crimes, but this man hasn't*
done anything wrong.'

⁴² *Then he said, 'Jesus, remember me when you come into*
your Kingdom.'

⁴³ *And Jesus replied, 'I assure you, today you will be*
with me in paradise.'

Luke 23:39–43

⌁Remember Me⌁

Dismas, the Believing Criminal

The crowd had kept a distance, waiting for
the spectacle to end. My blurred vision left
me without any sign of hope — this was my
wretched end.

Life was cheap, and here the soldiers were
looking to take the last of the raiment from the
dying and dead.

Four soldiers stood at the foot of the cross, arguing.

'It's mine — I've earned it!'
'You can't have it, you got it last time!'
'Give it to me, I could use one like that!'

They each agreed to one piece of the
Criminals clothing for themselves, however the
undergarment remained.

This was no ordinary loin-cloth.

It was woven and seamless from top to bottom —
Roman soldiers would hardly appreciate the cultural
and religious significance of this priestly garment,
given it was stripped from a dying Criminal, who
was to have no future use of it, shortly.

The exercise was merely social entertainment:
to humiliate the dying of their last possessions,
whilst stripped bare in the face of the world.

'I'll bet you for it.'
'Ok, I have a dice.'
'Right. Let's do this.'

All four rolled the dice. The one with the highest
number would take home the garment.

'OOOOHHH!'
'RATS!'
'WINNER!'

The winner was quickly decided, and the fate of
the under-garment was sealed.

The soldiers dispersed nearby, to feast their eyes
on the final hours of Life.

Turning to the crucified Criminal on my left,
His breathing was liquid-heavy, exhaling with

blood-filled lungs spattering the dregs of life into the clammy air.

Further to the left, there came a gush of abuse and ridicule, unbottled in a last-ditch effort to be unhitched from the world's stage:

'So you're the Messiah, are you?
Prove it by saving yourself —
    and us, too, while you're at it!'

Silence.

SILENCE!

Who can argue at a time like this?

Clearly, no-one was going anywhere.

The King had no intention of returning a word.

But *who were we* to expect salvation?

Who were we to demand our freedom?

We were criminals against the Empire, rebels against the Emperor. On all accounts, we knew what we were doing — *and we knew this would be our punishment if we were caught.*

I retorted, labouring under my breath:

Don't you fear G-d …
even when …
you have been …
sentenced to die?

We deserve …
to die …
for our crimes.
But this man …
hasn't done …
anything wrong.

Turning to the king of the Jews, I made my request:

Jesus …
remember me …
when you come …
into Your Kingdom.

With eyes full of compassion, turning to me,
Jesus replied:

I assure you …
today …
you will …
be with Me …
in paradise.

Via Crucis

Via Crucis 12:

Jesus' Mother and Brothers

25 *Standing near the cross were Jesus' mother, and his mother's sister Mary (the wife of Clopas), and Mary Magdalene.*

26 *When Jesus saw his mother standing there beside the disciple he loved, he said to her,*
'Dear woman, here is your son.'

27 *And he said to this disciple,*
'Here is your mother.'

And from then on this disciple took her into his home.

John 19:25–27

⸺𝒜 New Family⸺

Mary, Sister-in-Law to Jesus' Mother

Anguish gripped my heart. *This is the most dreadful day of my life.*

I can hardly describe my anger, my grief, my isolation … for my Nephew, whose heavy breathing and sighing from the cross echoed from above.

The darkness, *the darkness*, edged in and around us.

Heaven's eyes closed.

Forsaken.

Forgotten.

I had always trusted Yahweh to come through for us, to provide a Deliverer.

And yet, when the promise of salvation was in sight, it vanished, and my hopes were dashed.

This was the end.

And here we were waiting, at the foot of the cross: myself, Jesus' mother, and Jesus' friend Mary of Magdala.

Through the death of our spouses, we had become close; we had become *family*.

> My husband Alphaeus passed away, leaving our two boys James ('the Just') and Joseph under my care. Also, the brother of Mary's husband Joseph, *Clopas*, had lost his wife, leaving him to raise two boys: Simon and Jude. Through the course of time I found comfort and strength in Clopas, and after we wed we raised the four boys together.

> Later, when Mary (being the sister-in-law to Clopas) also lost Joseph, we made invitation for her and Jesus to join us.

> Our blended family shared the lodging as we supported each other: Clopas, Simon and Jude; myself with James and Joseph (whom we later called Joses to avoid confusion); and Mary with her son Jesus. In this way, the boys became family, and Jesus called them

His brothers. Although they were not entirely of the same flesh and blood, it's the way it worked at the time.

In all, we became a close-knit family; Clopas and I raised the five teenage boys with Mary. Those were full and happy days, despite the loss of our loved ones.

The Son — *our son* — was in His final minutes of life, hanging from that cross like a wretched criminal bleeding to death.

And yet His concern was not for His own life; He had a plan for everything, *and for everyone.*

Next to His mother stood *the beloved disciple*, with his mother Salome and Mary Magdalene. Calling to his mother, and motioning to the *disciple*, He said, 'Dear woman, here is your son.' The words of the Psalm came flooding into her mind, she knew that G-d *was setting the lonely into families.*

And turning to John, He said, 'Here is your mother.'

Their eyes, full of grief and gratitude, humbly accepted the new positions that they were led to take toward each other.

These last minutes of Life, this final earthly day, brought about a new beginning, and set up a new family.

Via Crucis 13:
Jesus and the Centurion

45   *At noon, darkness fell across the whole land until three o'clock.*

46   *At about three o'clock, Jesus called out with a loud voice, 'Eli, Eli, lema sabachthani?' which means 'My G-d, my G-d, why have you abandoned me?'*

47   *Some of the bystanders misunderstood and thought he was calling for the prophet Elijah.*

48   *One of them ran and filled a sponge with sour wine, holding it up to him on a reed stick so he could drink.*

49   *But the rest said, 'Wait! Let's see whether Elijah comes to save him.'*

50   *Then Jesus shouted out again, and he released his spirit.*

51   *At that moment the curtain in the sanctuary of the Temple was torn in two, from top to bottom.*

The earth shook, rocks split apart,

52 *and tombs opened.*

The bodies of many G-dly men and women who had died were raised from the dead.

53 *They left the cemetery after Jesus' resurrection, went into the holy city of Jerusalem, and appeared to many people.*

54 *The Roman officer and the other soldiers at the crucifixion were terrified by the earthquake and all that had happened.*

They said, 'This man truly was the Son of G-d!'

Matthew 27:45–54

~Surely~

Longinus, the Roman Centurion

Earlier in the day, Pilate had summonsed me to watch over the crucifixion. I took my men, and the five of us headed into the crowd fully armed.

The scene was one of total mayhem, and we were there to maintain some sort of order amongst it all.

By-passers from the crowd jeered.

> 'Ha! Look at you now!'
> 'You said you were going to destroy the
>   Temple and rebuild it in three days.'
> 'If you are the Son of G-d, save yourself
>   and come down from the cross!'
> 'He saved others, let him save himself if
>   he is really G-d's Messiah, the Chosen One.'

Envious priests and the religious elite hurled their
mockery at the dying.

> 'He saved others, but he can't save himself!'
> 'Let this Messiah, this king of Israel,
>   come down from the cross so we can see it
>   and believe Him.'
> 'He trusted G-d, let G-d rescue him now
>   if he wants him.'

A group of grief laden women, in tears, watched
from a distance. They had cared for Him, but
now were helpless.

The mother of the Criminal in the centre pressed
in for her last words, before his curtain would fall.

'STAY BACK!' I issued the command to the
taunting onlookers and bystanders. The mother
had a right to say her good-byes, but I needed to
keep order.

Eerily, a thick darkness enveloped us. The sun
stopped shining. I felt a tingling up my spine which
worked its way up until a sordid vulgar repulsive
essence of dread rose to the base of my skull.

Heaven and earth trembled at this sight — what
had we done to incur the wrath of the gods?
Days like this had been mentioned in the Temple

of Zeus, and today demonstrated that there was more to what we see on this earthly plane.

A quiet hush enveloped the crowd. No-one moved.

The agonising breaths of those crucified were the only noises that were audible from above the crowd.

Words of despair rang from the central cross.

> 'My G-d.
> My G-d.
> Why did you abandon Me?'

Some of those standing by thought he was calling for the prophet Elijah.

Three hours passed until the suns light was restored. As the fog lifted, turning to me, our eyes locked, and He requested a drink, 'I'm thirsty.'

I indicated to my men, and they brought over the bucket drugged with sour wine that He had refused to accept earlier. The sponge was dipped in, and the reed stick lifted up for the Victim's last drink.

My men joined in the ridicule along with the crowd.

> 'If you are the king of the Jews,
>   then save yourself!'

A series of heavy sighs echoed from the cross.

Finally, the death of Jesus ended with a loud shout.

'Father, into Your hands I trust my spirit.'

Silence.

The crowd hushed at the spectacle.

Sullen faces of pitiful women full of disbelief watched on.

Birds stopped twittering.

This was the end.

At that moment, the earth shook violently, back and forth; large rocks split apart. The crowd ran in terror from the scene, looking for cover. Divine judgement had been declared, and the earth lay witness to this.

In all my time as Centurion, I had never experienced such a sight.

It was terrifying. Even my men trembled in fear — *nothing shakes a Roman soldier on duty.*

This indeed was a Divine event.

I faced him as He died, and to say the least, it was not normal.

Looking into the sky, I searched for meaning. What had we witnessed? What had we done?

The sun broke through the gloom, striking my face, illuminating my heart and mind. I was filled with a fresh sense of meaning, a revelation of the events that had unfolded.

'Surely!'

I was not trained to think like this. It came from outside me.

'SURELY!'

My mind raced back through what had happened, from the Praetorium to the Skull; the mockery from the crowd, the priests and the soldiers.

Could it be that we were wrong after all? All of us?

'Surely this man was innocent?'

Maybe this was all staged?

> The priests had led with a sense of
>   cruel intent.
> The Governor was manipulated
>   into subservient submission.
> The Jewish calendar focused on the death
>   of an innocent lamb.

The Victim seemed to facilitate the time
and actions of his own demise.

And on this historic day, I was called to
ensure that the event was handled smoothly
and without fault.

Suddenly, it all made sense.

This wasn't some random killing or selfish desire
for control by the leading priests.

Here was the redemption of the world,
the sacrifice that would restore us to G-d.

'SURELY.'

I was filled with deep conviction. What else could
it have been?

'THIS MAN TRULY WAS THE SON OF G-D!'

Via Crucis 14:
Jesus Placed in the Tomb

⁵⁷ *As evening approached, Joseph, a rich man from Arimathea who had become a follower of Jesus,*

⁵⁸ *went to Pilate and asked for Jesus' body. And Pilate issued an order to release it to him.*

⁵⁹ *Joseph took the body and wrapped it in a long sheet of clean linen cloth.*

⁶⁰ *He placed it in his own new tomb, which had been carved out of the rock. Then he rolled a great stone across the entrance and left.*

⁶¹ *Both Mary Magdalene and the other Mary were sitting across from the tomb and watching.*

Matthew 27:57–61

⁓It Is Finished⁓

Joseph, the Religious Leader

I hadn't slept for two days.

Physical exhaustion and fatigue started to get to me, and in my whole being I felt crushed under the weight of what I had been through.

> Last night the chief priest called a hasty council meeting. It was the day of preparation for our annual feast, and the request had come through a messenger. We were called to meet at the house of Annas, father-in-law of Caiaphas the high priest, to be briefed on the Passover proceedings, and *to take care of another matter that had arisen.*
>
> It was late, and the request came unexpectedly to my door. There was a certain haste in the

messenger's voice, and I was wary of what could be going on. 'I'll be right there,' I motioned, and started to pack my things.

Arriving in the darkness, the house was stirred with angry outbursts, and accusations. I stepped forward to peer through the front door, *what was all this commotion about?*

Inside, there was the Man, Jesus.

He was bound with restraints so that He couldn't forge an escape. Not that He wanted to.

The ruckus emanated from some sort of exploratory pre-trial, seeking grounds by way of confession that Jesus might condemn Himself. Not that it would ever eventuate to anything — my fellow Pharisees and members of the Sanhedrin could never find grounds to kill a fellow Jew, let alone this good Man.

The late hour turned into the early morning, and the pre-trial proved futile.

'Enough! To the Sanhedrin!' yelled Annas, clearly annoyed that a confession did not convey any useful legal hinge so as to condemn the Man.

Pushing Him forward, they dragged Jesus down the path to the high priest's residence. The real trial was about to begin. The religious judge and jury were all present and accounted for. All we needed was a solid verdict, and an executioner.

'Bring forward the witnesses!' Caiaphas was insistent on making this a quick affair.

The leading priests and the entire high council searched for those who could lie about Jesus in order to put Him to death.

'We heard him say, "I will destroy this temple made with human hands and in three days I will build another, made without human hands." Although this gained the support of many of the council, their stories did not align.

To gain a ruling for the death penalty wasn't easy. According to our Law, a person could only be put to death on the account of two or three witnesses. And in this case, there were no consistent testimonies to make it happen.

Not that I was in support of their decision, having listened to His teachings and seen the mighty miracles. As I was a member of the Sanhedrin, I had become a *secret believer* and supporter of Jesus. And not just me, but Nicodemus, my fellow council member and Pharisee, was also a secret disciple. Together we had spent many hours discussing whether this Man really was the promised Messiah. We were believers.

During these accusations and fabricated stories, we argued that Jesus was not who they were making Him out to be. Notably, our voices were drowned out.

Again, the trial proved futile.

Again, more accusations were thrown at Jesus — yet He cared not for the audience.

Daylight broke into the courtroom. The high priest needed a verdict, or all this was in vain.

Almost screaming at the top of his voice, Caiaphas demanded,
'I invoke the name of the living G-d: TELL US IF YOU ARE THE MESSIAH, THE SON OF G-D!'

Silence.

Eyes darted around the room toward one another. *Was He going to answer the high priest?*

The reply was firm, yet humble, 'You have said it. From now on you will see the Son of Man seated in the place of power at G-d's right hand and coming on the clouds of heaven.'

Tearing his clothes in horror, Caiaphas gleefully claimed the legal charge against the Man.

'Blasphemy!'
'BLASPHEMY!'

'You yourselves have heard it. Why do we need any more witnesses?'

'WHAT'S YOUR VERDICT?'

A breakthrough, this is what they were waiting for. The Man was clearly guilty by His own admission, breaking the Law, without need of any further witnesses.

The crowd jeered joyously, 'GUILTY!' 'HE DESERVES TO DIE!'

I couldn't help but to think that I'd failed. Suddenly grief had overcome me, and I couldn't stand to be with those who had been my spiritual family for all my adult life. I had to leave and escape this madness.

That was last night, and now, here we were at the foot of the Cross. It was the end of a long and blood-thirsty day, and they got what they wanted — to be rid of the Man, once and for all.

My grief and sadness were overwhelming; there was nothing I could have done to prevent this, but I wanted to do more. I wanted to show my respect and condolences to the family and friends that were watching the episode in disbelief.

Over the years, and through my wealthy connections, I had found favour with the rulers of the Roman government and our religious leaders: To say that I was well connected would be an understatement. And looking up at the disfigured body of Jesus on the cross as the sun fell towards the horizon gave me an opportunity to demonstrate the deep respect that I had for the Man. I decided to take a risk which would expose me as an open believer, no longer as a secret disciple — I went to see Pilate personally for the release.

'What do you mean, "He's dead"?' quizzed Pilate. *Criminals don't die this quickly.*

'Get me Longinus!' Pilate needed to verify this and see if this was true before He would release the body. Although we were friends, as Roman Governor he was required to follow protocol.

Ten minutes later, the Roman officer appeared.

'Sir — yes — I can confirm that Jesus has died.' The soldier was in shock, having closely witnessed the events.

'He's yours.' Pilate nodded to me, handing over the body for burial.

'Thank you, sir.'

And with that, I hastily made my way to pick up Nicodemus and the embalming spices. I would need help to take the Body down from the cross, and shift it to the tomb.

Arriving together we brought the cross to the ground. Roman soldiers were guarding the executions, and we requested their tools to remove the hefty nails from the hands and feet of the Dead.

> Before we started the task, we took a long look at the One who had been our inspirer for the last few years. His words rang in our ears, and our hearts had been moved by what He said. With His touch he had healed and restored many peoples infirmities; and with a command He told demons to leave.

This surely was not simply a good man
that fell into the wrong hands; this was the
Messiah, the Saviour of the world. And with
His death our hopes were now diminished.
The light of the world was extinguished.

Proceeding with the task, we unhinged the nails
from His hands and feet. The burial cloth was in
the form of a long sheet that we spread out on
the ground nearby, and we rolled the Body onto
it, taping in the sides of the sheet around the
head, arms and feet to make moving it easier. It
would take both of us to relocate the body to its
final resting place, each of us taking hold of an
end of the corpse.

We headed to my pre-cut tomb which was
nearby. It was located in a nearby garden for
my own future use, and I had paid a pricey sum
for it. I wanted it to be a place of reflection and
solemnity for family and friends who were to
come and pay their respects, and the surrounding
gardens provided a space for privacy during their
times of grief.

We brought the Body inside the tomb; it was cold
and dark, and a long carved table was available
to facilitate the embalming process where the
body would be prepared. Rolling back the sheet,

we started sprinkling and rubbing the spices
that Nicodemus had brought onto the fleshy
surface. We needed to act quickly; there was now
no natural light to facilitate this process, and the
Sabbath was about to begin — when the last of
the sun's rays fell below the horizon.

It became evident that we were not able to
finish in time, and we would need to come back
on Sunday morning, so we folded the cloth
back around the Body and placed a fresh towel
covering His head.

Before we left, we took one last gaze at what was
our Saviour, our promised hope.

This does not feel right.

But we knew there was nothing else we could do;
nothing we could do further *today*.

The large stone that was to seal the entrance to
the tomb was outside, resting on a slight incline,
and which would roll into position once the
supporting pin was removed. It was carved out
of rock to make the task of sealing the tomb so
much easier, firming up the tomb entrance once it
was laid in place. It was not easily removed — the
sheer weight of the rock, along with the incline,
made it quite a job for a number of people to

have to roll it back up the incline, where it also had to be re-secured, before access could be gained to the entrance.

Releasing the pin, we let the stone roll into position, the last rays of sunshine ebbed behind the horizon, and the Sabbath began.

A number of women — close friends and family members of Jesus — were there, consoling each other. Mary Magdalene, and the other Mary, and the women from Galilee who had looked after Jesus during His ministry years in that region were also there.

Fatigued, we headed back home.

There was really nothing more we could do.

We left speechless.

Was this really the end?

Via Crucis

Selah

⁓My Eulogy⁓

Jesus, the Life

Rejected
I grew up in a small town
Everyone knew
I was the son of an unwed mum.

Mum and dad,
Not yet married,
'It's a boy,' they cried
With tears of joy, but feared my fate.

Friends,
Those boys I grew up with
Eyed me suspiciously,
Never trusting, not completely,
Though My brothers and sisters were 'normal'
   to them.

At my *coming of age* day
No-one came, no-one sang, no-one danced.
They knew — *they knew* — and they rejected Me.

So I grew up despised among My friends.
Their parents often joked about Me,
'Joseph's son', from Nazareth.

Rejected. Despised. Hated.

And here in this cold stone tomb
My body lay wrapped in cloths,
Where six hours earlier
My exposed flesh dying on a cross.

My Father, that booming voice,
From heaven, had endorsed me just three years ago,
This is My Beloved Son,
In whom I am well pleased.'

But today, as darkness closed in,
I cried, *'Father, why have you forsaken Me?'*

And there, My spirit was broken.
My body lay crushed.
And heaven's eyes closed.

Rejected.
Rejected by man
Rejected by G-d

Despised in My death
Hated by the world.

And yet … *I Am Life*.

Via Lucis 1:

Jesus Rises From the Dead

5   *Then the angel spoke to the women. 'Don't be afraid!' he said. 'I know you are looking for Jesus, who was crucified.*

6   *He isn't here! He is risen from the dead, just as he said would happen. Come, see where his body was lying.*

Matthew 28:5–7

⁓A New Beginning⁓

The Other Mary

It was still dark, the first day of the week, and my intrepid team of closely-knit women headed through the dark streets to the burial garden. We had witnessed where they laid Christ's body; despite the early morning light, we made no mistake how to get back to it; we were here to pay our final respects and farewell the Dead.

We ventured past the deathly scenes from just two days previous, the mound of dirt called skull hill — where legend has it that Goliath's skull is buried — and paused before entering the garden clearing to be confronted with a sickly emotion that we hadn't quite worked through up until this point: *Who was going to roll the stone away?*

We stopped.

Need we go any farther?

We had heard from the priests that a temple guard had been assigned to the tomb, *just in case the disciples come to steal the body away, and tell everybody that He was raised from the dead!*

Seriously — *do they really expect that we would concoct such an elaborate hoax?* Our Master, our Leader, was dead. But it wasn't in us to propagate lies. We were women in mourning.

The sweet aroma from the nard perfume and burial spices caught my attention while we waited for the group decision to move forward. We had waited over 24 hours after the killing — until sundown on the Sabbath — to go buy spices, so that we could anoint Jesus' body at the next opportunity. That was 12 hours ago, and we hadn't slept all night — eager with anticipation, but also consoling each other through this time of grief.

Mary, from Magdala, caught our attention. She was a born leader, able to command a troop, and kept us together during our time of grief and mourning. The Lord had touched her marvellously, expelling seven demons from her and freeing her to think for herself. She felt deeply indebted, proving it wherever she went by her loyal devotion and assistance whenever and wherever she could.

But for me, I could hardly look up.

Jesus wasn't just a Rabbi or Teacher, He was family, indeed, the son of my husbands' brother. He had grown up in my house, and like His own mother I was considered a mother to him. My children were his brothers and sisters. We looked out for Him, knowing Him to be strong in character, and we didn't want to see Him go the way of the Zealots. There were many revolutionaries that ended up dead. My heart stopped beating at the thought of this — *was I wrong all along?*

In this momentary pause, the ground started to shake — just like it did during that fateful afternoon with those bodies on the cross. As the earth quaked, the guards fell to the ground dead, frozen in fear. What was going on?

Suddenly a brilliant light, as of a thousand suns, radiated upon the tomb, filling the darkness void with light.

It was an angel.

We hid our eyes; it was too much to take in.

The glistening heavenly being descended upon the large stone that was the only relic guarding the entrance, rolled it aside, and sat upon it.

The sight was dazzling.

We were left dumbfounded, speechless.

The angels' clothes were white, whiter than any cleansing agent that we had used, and sparkled in the early dawn. The radiance was celestial, breaking through the heavens it made us tingle with delight and wonder.

We wondered what was happening, or was about to happen. We held our distance for a while, awkwardly wondering how to take the next step.

The sun started breaking through the trees of the garden, although light was not necessary due to the luminescence that emanated from the angel.

Our hesitant pause had caused us to become cautious. We didn't want to race ahead lest there be other powerful heavenly beings that might not be as kind; and we certainly didn't want to come across any more panic-stricken guards or religious leaders that might want to finish the job, or who might try to kill us as well.

'Ladies, don't be afraid,' called the angel. 'I know you are looking for Jesus, who was crucified.'

'He isn't here! He is risen from the dead, just as He said would happen. Come, see where His body was lying.'

Mary gave an excited nod towards us, and we crept forward towards the tomb. We came not expecting it to be empty; we had come looking for a Body, to perform *the task*, the ritual, and to say our last good-byes.

We were not ready for what would happen next.

As we entered the tomb, our hearts leaped again and we went into shock — gasping for air.

Inside, a young man was sitting to the right of where the Body lay. He was dressed in a white robe, but not as shiny as the angel that sat on the stone. He looked sort of *ordinary*.

Again, *what was this?*

We had enough surprises for one day; our emotions were not ready for these events.

The young man gave a simple explanation, as one who had just received a message from the heavenly being. He tried hard to reassure us, being fully convinced at what was happening inside the tomb.

'Don't be alarmed. You are looking for Jesus of Nazareth, who was crucified. He isn't here! He is risen from the dead! Look, this is the place where they laid his body.'

We honestly did not know what to think. Our minds were racing, our senses overloaded with fear and hope. Outside, an angel; inside, a man. It was all too much to take in at once.

'Go and tell His disciples, including Peter, that Jesus is going ahead of you to Galilee. You will see Him there, just as He told you before He died.' The instructions came with a sense of purpose, but were these words coming from a reliable source?

All this will have a natural explanation soon.

We looked around the tomb. He was right. *There was no Body on the bench that we had expected to find there.* The burial cloths had been rolled up and set aside; and the tomb now opened up with fragrant spices, giving off a sense of new life.

This is a place of birth, not a burial ground.

All of this was confusing.

We didn't understand.

Our minds were numb with the realisation that
this newfound mystery was no game of shadows.

> *Is this vision of the angel real?*
> *Can we trust the words that the angel —*
>   *and the young man — spoke to us?*
> *Should we be feeling relieved at not seeing the Body?*
> *Why do we tremble with fear at the sight*
>   *of those guards, fallen to the ground?*

'Go on to Galilee. You will see Him there.
Remember what I have told you,' the angel
reassured us.

But we were bewildered.

We needed to escape, to find the men who could
help bring all this together.

Running, no, *fleeing*, from the tomb, past the angel,
past the hill of death, we made it home.

Nothing of all we said made sense to the others.

All they could glean from us was that the tomb
was open, the body of Jesus had gone missing,
and some crazy women were terrified and
distressed at these events.

Slowing down, and taking deep breaths, I managed to calm myself down after the run.

I was bewildered, but full of joy.

Perhaps, PERHAPS, this was a new beginning.

Via Lucis

Via Lucis 2:
Jesus' Empty Tomb

1   *Early on Sunday morning, as the new day was dawning, Mary Magdalene and the other Mary went out to visit the tomb.*

2   *Suddenly there was a great earthquake! For an angel of the Lord came down from heaven, rolled aside the stone, and sat on it.*

3   *His face shone like lightning, and his clothing was as white as snow.*

4   *The guards shook with fear when they saw him, and they fell into a dead faint.*

5   *Then the angel spoke to the women. 'Don't be afraid!' he said. 'I know you are looking for Jesus, who was crucified.*

6   *He isn't here! He is risen from the dead, just as he said would happen. Come, see where his body was lying.*

7   *And now, go quickly and tell his disciples that he has
     risen from the dead, and he is going ahead of you to
     Galilee. You will see him there. Remember what I
     have told you.'*

Matthew 28:1–7

Don't Be Afraid

The Angel on the Stone

With Wisdom, I was there when He laid the foundations of the earth, right by His side. Together we saw the formation of all things.

From the chaos and void emerged the entwinement of heaven and earth, a brilliantly connected world. Nothing, NOTHING, would separate the love of the Creator from His creation. His breath infused the heavenly, spiritual and unseen eternal life force into the physical, earthly and natural realm. And it glowed, resonating with the brilliance and power of Almighty G-d.

The Lord looked at all the work of His hands, and said, 'It is good.' Wisdom smiled, and I laughed; together we drew in all that was made, fully satisfying all our senses.

With Hagar, I was there when she fled from the mistreatment of her mistress. She was crying, heart-broken, and had lost hope. Although she was a slave to Sarai, I told her to return, and to submit to her, with the blessing that 'your descendants will be too many to count.'

As the Lord's angel, I brought hope, and gave her the blessing that the descendants of her son would multiply, being too numerous to count. His name would be Ishmael, meaning that G-d hears the broken hearted.

With Abraham, I was there when he drew the knife to slay his son, his only son whom he loved, as a sacrifice on Mount Moriah. He was faithful, and obedient, ready to give away the child of promise — not withholding it from the Lord. I called out to him, 'Abraham — do not lay a hand on the boy. Now I know that you fear G-d, because you have not withheld from me your son, your only son.'

As the Lord's angel, I brought the sacrifice, substituting his one and only son, and placed a ram in the thicket behind him. So Abraham called that place, *The Lord will provide.*

With Rebekah, I was there when the servant came to find a wife for Abraham's son Isaac. I led them hand in hand to find each other — a perfect match!

With Moses, I was sent ahead of him to bring the nation of Israel out of Egypt. I appeared as flames in the burning bush, and made him the ruler and judge of Israel. With mighty signs and wonders, I brought the Egyptians to nothing, slaying their first born, and crushing their armies. I was a pillar of cloud to guide the Lord's people by day, and a pillar of fire to give them light, so that they could travel by day or by night.

With Gideon, I brought the Midianites to an end with just 300 men. I accepted his offering — the unleavened bread and the broth — and consumed it with the tip of my staff. And together we broke the taunts of those who dared to come against the people of the Lord, the Captain of the Host of Israel.

With Elijah, the prophet was running scared for his life, and sat under a tree to die. He fell asleep with exhaustion, when I woke him up to eat and drink, and to send him on his way. There he came to the mountain of G-d and spent the night in a cave, when he presented his case to the Lord.

On the mountain, before the Lord, a powerful
wind tore the mountains apart, and shattered
the rocks. An earthquake split the ground, and a
blazing fire burst forth. And then in the stillness,
a gentle whisper was heard.

With David, I was angered by the census he had
taken, and I stretched out my hand to release
a plague to destroy Jerusalem. My people, the
Lord's people, were like sheep to be slaughtered,
and David recanted his actions to me.

At the threshing floor of Araunah the Jebusite I
stopped, and withheld the anger of the Lord, and
David built there an altar.

With Shadrach, Meshach and Abednego, I walked
in the flames with them so that their clothes were
not burnt, nor the smell of smoke found on
them. They defied the kings command and were
willing to give up their lives rather than serve or
worship any G-d except their own.

With Daniel, I shut the mouths of lions
because he was innocent in the sight of the
Lord. Although he was thrown in alive at the
king's command, he was not touched, and his
perpetrators instead paid the price.

With Zechariah, I heard the prayer for his wife Elizabeth to bear a child, and I honoured it. Although at first he did not believe, he soon learned that G-d could be trusted, and he named the child John — just as he had been commanded.

With Mary, I was sent to Nazareth with a message to the one who bore much favour. She believed, saying, 'I am the Lord's servant — may your words be fulfilled.' Although she was a virgin, the Holy Spirit came upon her and the power of the Most High overshadowed her, and she bore the Son of G-d.

With Joseph, he was a devout and righteous man, not wanting to make a public disgrace of his pregnant fiancé. I appeared to him in a dream and explained that Mary was carrying the Lord's child, and that there was nothing to fear. He was to take her as his wife, because what was conceived in her was from the Holy Spirit.

Later, I warned Joseph, again in a dream, warning him to flee to Egypt, as the ruler Herod was searching for the child to kill him. And when Herod died, I again appeared to Joseph in a dream, while in Egypt, to let them know that it was safe for them to return to their land.

With Jesus, I was at His side in the garden of Gethsemane, when He prayed that the cup of wrath be taken away. His sweaty prayers dripped of blood, and I strengthened Him that He might not falter in his mission.

The next day I was there as they drove in the Roman nails of death that secured Him to the cross. And at midday, I was there when the Father's face was turned away, and the place grew cold and dark. At the end, I was there, with the earthquake that shook the ground, as the spirit of the Lord was handed back to the Father who gave it, where the temple veil was torn and heaven rejoined earth in a forever victory.

And today, here I am, at the opening of the tomb. Again, the earth quaked at this event and all creation stood still and trembled.

Through all of time I've been waiting for this day, this time of redemption. A time that marked a new beginning, the ultimate victory of light over darkness, taken up in residence by the Lord of heaven and earth.

This time it was not just another angelic visit to point the way; this time I was tasked to release the Life, to declare that there was no longer victory in death:

Where O Death is your victory? Where O Death
is your sting?
The perishable has been clothed with the imperishable!
The mortal has been clothed with immortality!
Death has been swallowed up in victory!

Today, the women came searching the tomb,
searching for the Body, but they didn't find it.

'Don't be afraid! I know you are looking
for Jesus, who was crucified.
He isn't here! He is risen from the dead,
just as He said would happen.
Come, see where His body was lying.'

Via Lucis 3:
Jesus Appears to Mary Magdalene

11 *Mary was standing outside the tomb crying, and as she wept, she stooped and looked in.*

12 *She saw two white-robed angels, one sitting at the head and the other at the foot of the place where the body of Jesus had been lying.*

13 *'Dear woman, why are you crying?' the angels asked her. 'Because they have taken away my Lord,' she replied, 'and I don't know where they have put him.'*

14 *She turned to leave and saw someone standing there. It was Jesus, but she didn't recognize him.*

15 *'Dear woman, why are you crying?' Jesus asked her. 'Who are you looking for?'*
She thought he was the gardener. 'Sir,' she said, 'if you have taken him away, tell me where you have put him, and I will go and get him.'

16   *'Mary!' Jesus said.*
She turned to him and cried out, 'Rabboni!' (which is
Hebrew for 'Teacher').

17   *'Don't cling to me,' Jesus said, 'for I haven't yet*
ascended to the Father. But go find my brothers and
tell them, 'I am ascending to my Father and your
Father, to my G-d and your G-d.''

John 20:11–17

Why Are You Crying?

Mary, of Magdala

I was the leader of the Myrrhbearers, the group of Galilean women who were planning to make our way at the first light of day to the tomb. As required by law, we had waited until sundown the night before to purchase more spices, and which we had prepared overnight, to complete the burial ritual. We had hardly slept, our grief was shrouded with the excitement of the planned visitation to the tomb.

With me came Salome and *the other Mary* to where we saw Him laid. We were careful with each step so as not to fall or stumble. Our feet felt frail and were shaken by the events of the last few days.

Encroaching the garden entrance, our hearts thumped in our chests. *All our hopes had been dashed within hours, coming to a tumultuous end, when Jesus was placed into this dark cold tomb.*

We were grieving; all our loyalties had been tied to His teaching, His kindness, and His acts of power. We were convinced that He was the Son of G-d, the Saviour of the world. And yet, the morning mist hid our dreams among the gardens in silence.

> I dreamed of the time that He freed me, with a firm and authoritative voice, speaking directly into my being with deep care and attention. My heart skipped a beat, knowing that I was freed from the demons that had tormented me for many years.
>
> *I'm not the woman that I was before; I am now valued, precious, loved and honoured.*

But here in this garden there was barely sunlight, and gloomy shadows.

> Suddenly, an angel appeared, rolling the stone away, and sitting on it. The tomb was open! Shadows dispersed as heavenly light broke the morning sky. 'Behold, you are looking for Jesus who was crucified. He is not here. He is risen

from the dead, just as He said would happen. Come, see where His body was laying.'

Inside, the Body was gone; the burial cloths folded up. A young man in white linen also explained the mystery, echoing the angels words, and said we would see him in Galilee.

This was too much to take in.

We fled.
We screamed.
We told no-one.

Waiting, hiding, we conferred together, thinking about what to do. We couldn't go back home just yet, as the encounter we had just experienced had significantly changed the course of events that we had planned. Finally, catching our breath, we decided to cautiously return to the tomb, a second time.

Entering in, we didn't find the body of the Lord where we expected it to be laid. As we were puzzling over this, two men in dazzling clothes appeared and explained about the betrayal, the crucifixion and the resurrection of Jesus. *Then we remembered what Jesus had said to us back in Galilee.*

We rushed back to the eleven apostles-in-hiding and everyone else to tell them what had happened. Staying indoors, they planned to quietly disband their loyalties to each other, and go back to their trades.

But when we entered, we were bursting to tell our stories, which seemed like nonsense to these unconvinced disciples. While one was fervently telling her story, another would break in to tell her side, and to fill in the rest.

To everyone, it just made no sense at all. In fact, there was no credibility to our stories — it just left people confused.

To everyone's astonishment, Peter jumped up, along with John, and ran. Where were they going? What were they hoping to find? Did they want to believe?

I trailed behind, the men travelling so much faster by foot than I could carry myself, and I arrived a little while later, back to where we were at daybreak.

Peter went in and saw the wrapped linen lying there, with the cloth that held Jesus' head folded up and lying apart from the other wrappings. Puzzled, he wondered what it all meant — he did not understand what had happened, or what was written in the scriptures. Next John entered the tomb, and he saw and believed. Until then, they hadn't understood that Jesus must rise from the dead. Then they left for home.

Meanwhile, I stood outside at the tomb.

This was my Lord, my Master, the One who demonstrated great love and care for me. I had pledged to stay by His side and care for Him — along with my friends Joanna, Mary and others who cared for His needs while in Galilee.

The thought of this great loss made my head spiral; for years we had worked hard to maintain the ministry as Jesus shared about the Kingdom of G-d — and yet now our dreams lay shattered. It was all too much. I broke down and wept.

Wiping away the tears, I yearned for another look inside the tomb. Maybe they couldn't find what they were looking for? Maybe it was too dark and they couldn't see Him? Maybe they just didn't try hard enough?

The thoughts circling my mind warred against my emotions, dragging me down. I simply needed answers, as none of this made sense. So I stepped in again, inside the tomb, just for one last look.

Breaking through the tears, an angel sat at each of the head and the foot of where the body of

Jesus once lay. They were compassionate, and the energy of heaven flowed through the room when they spoke.

'Why are you crying?' they asked.

I pulled myself together to provide an answer, not entirely sure if it would help bring back the Saviour whom I longed for, 'They have taken away my Lord, and I don't know where they have put Him.'

At this my heart burst, and I fell to the ground again, unable to control the depths of sorrow that ebbed from my heart. I was soaked in the pain of loss and the agony of grief, and not even heaven could relieve my anguish.

Dragging myself forward towards the entrance, I felt helpless, hopeless, and useless. My life was a waste, and nothing could change that. Ahead of me, in the garden, a figure emerged, waiting outside. I dared not lift my head towards him, and I cared not to answer any more questions. Not from him, nor anyone else. All I wanted to do was go home and die; life was not worth the pain of this loss.

The gardener enquired of me, 'Dear woman, why are you crying? Who are you looking for?'

I dared not look. I did not want to answer. But I sensed that genuine care was being offered, and that it would be rude not to reply.

'Dear sir, if you have taken him away, please tell me where he is, and I will go and get him.'

Now that didn't come out right. My grief-stricken state made no sense at all to the man. What would I do with the body once I received it? Was I to keep this to myself?

I couldn't see. I couldn't breathe. I couldn't even form simple sentences to make meaningful words. If only Jesus were here to console me, and make things right. Then I could see, then I could rejoice where others were confused or dismayed.

I was about to leave. No-one needs to see a weeping woman, howling over the loss of her dead friend.

Then a change began.
Time slowed down.

I could sense that the hands of heaven's clock had stopped, and my soul was longing for a reply from this stranger.

Why was he staring at me? Why didn't he want to move out of the way?

Sunlight broke through, splashing me on my face.

'Mary!'

A familiar voice.
A *very familiar* voice.

But no, it couldn't be.
And yet, my heart leapt at the thought.

Maybe my ears were deceiving me?
Was it really … the voice of the Lord?

Turning back I caught a full view of the risen
Lord, the Teacher, exclaiming, 'Rabboni!'

Running, I clung to Him.
I was never to let Him go.

Moments passed in our embrace.
And inside that small frame of time came relief,
healing, and fullness.

Holding hands, He let me go, and asked me to do
the same.

'Please, go find my brothers and tell them that I
am ascending to Mmy Father and your Father, to
My G-d and to your G-d.'

And with a flash, He was out of sight.

Via Lucis 4:
Jesus and the Disciples

18 *Mary Magdalene found the disciples and told them, 'I have seen the Lord!' Then she gave them his message.*

19 *That Sunday evening the disciples were meeting behind locked doors because they were afraid of the Jewish leaders.*
Suddenly, Jesus was standing there among them!
'Peace be with you,' he said.

20 *As he spoke, he showed them the wounds in his hands and his side. They were filled with joy when they saw the Lord!*

John 20:18–20

‿From Fear to Joy‿

James, the Greater

It made no sense at all.

Mary ran bursting into the room, excited yet scared, along with the other Galilean women, and they all blurted out together, all at once.

> 'The Lord has risen.'
> 'There was a shining angel sitting up
>   on the stone.'
> 'There was a man inside the tomb.'
> 'The stone was rolled away.'
> 'There were two angels sitting inside the tomb.'
> 'There were two men in dazzling clothes
>   at the tomb.'
> 'They told us to go and wait at Galilee,
>   and He will come to us there.'

Each one talking over the other — it was nothing short of confusion. Clearly they were disturbed *by something*, and we couldn't make head nor tail of what they tried to say.

As the ladies continued their frantic talk, my mind drifted back over the events of the last few years, where I was privileged to be close to Jesus — part of His inner circle — and honoured to bear witness to many great and astonishing miracles.

> Fishermen by trade, we were preparing our nets ready to head out to the water for the day, when Jesus called me — along with my brother John — telling us not to be afraid, but to come and follow Him. 'Come with Me, and I'll make you fish for people!'
>
> I recalled when the Master called us 'sons of thunder'; complimenting us on our faith; but later gave us a stern rebuke when we wanted to call down fire from heaven on the Samaritan village that refused to welcome us.
>
> We were there at the house of Jairus, when the people were wailing and the dead girl lay silently in her bed — the screams of despair from family and friends were distressing. Despite the obvious facts, Jesus put the rest of the people outside, and with just me and

John and Peter, He brought her back to life
and handed her back to her grateful — yet
astonished — parents.

One day Jesus took us up the mountain
to pray. And doing so, we saw His clothes
change to dazzling white, and the appearance
of his face changed with the glow of heaven.
The light was so intense we couldn't bear
to watch, and we fell to the ground with
drowsiness. We saw His glory, and the two
witnesses — Moses and Elijah — discussing
His departure that He was to bring to
fulfillment at Jerusalem. Later, we felt the
significance of this so deeply that we asked
to sit at Jesus' left and right hands when He
returned to enter the heavenly glory.

And I recalled when we approached Him
about the destruction of Jerusalem, and He
gave us a private lesson about the end of the
world. Jesus gave us explicit details of the
things to come, and that we were to be on
guard against evil times ahead.

Then just three nights ago, Jesus took us with
Him, in private prayers and groans, in the
olive grove, to help pray through the final
hours of His life on earth. We didn't know it

then, and we were scared of what happened
next, what transpired through the arrest, the
crucifixion, and the burial. Our bones shook
to the core, and we ran away, lest we too
be found guilty of an uprising or rebellion
against Caesar.

The doors were locked, and we had huddled in
a secret place, a place of quiet, hoping to avoid
discovery. Even the temple priests were sure to be
on the lookout for trouble makers that dared to
start a religious rebellion against their Sanhedrin
and established laws. So we stayed inside, hoping
that all would return to normal, and we could go
back to our nets.

The message from these delirious women was
unnerving, and none of it made sense.

None of it made sense.

My thoughts lingered. *Was I going crazy?*

There was no way I could work out what was
going on, it was all too terrifying.

Suddenly, a brilliant light appeared, and the
commotion stopped. We all looked upon the Man
who stood in front of us. *Speechless.*

Breathing on us, His spirit calmed our fears and silenced the room. His words made all our natural earthly worries fade to nothing, and we basked in the glory of heavenly peace.

Our hearts paused to soak up His presence.

Holding out His hands, the wounds on His hands and side were evident; we could see where the spear had been thrust into His side, and the nail scars in His hands. This Jesus, this Living One, standing before us, was living proof that He who was declared dead *is now alive*.

Though we couldn't believe it, *we had to believe it* — though some of our party were not there for this visit. There was no question about the Evidence who stood before us all, to see with our eyes and touch with our hands.

But *more than this*, we weren't just seeing with our natural eyes, we were able to see with our heart.

Our hearts flooded with the peace of heaven, knowing that this Man, this Son of G-d, had indeed risen to Eternal Life.

And this is what we declare to you about *the Word of Life*.

Via Lucis 5:
Jesus on the Road to Emmaus

13   *That same day two of Jesus' followers were walking to the village of Emmaus, seven miles from Jerusalem.*

14   *As they walked along they were talking about everything that had happened.*

15   *As they talked and discussed these things, Jesus himself suddenly came and began walking with them.*

16   *But G-d kept them from recognizing him.*

17   *He asked them, 'What are you discussing so intently as you walk along?'*
   They stopped short, sadness written across their faces.

18   *Then one of them, Cleopas, replied, 'You must be the only person in Jerusalem who hasn't heard about all the things that have happened there the last few days.'*

19 *'What things?' Jesus asked.*
'The things that happened to Jesus, the man from
Nazareth,' they said. 'He was a prophet who did
powerful miracles, and he was a mighty teacher in the
eyes of G-d and all the people.

20 *But our leading priests and other religious leaders*
handed him over to be condemned to death, and they
crucified him.

21 *We had hoped he was the Messiah who had come to*
rescue Israel. This all happened three days ago.

22 *'Then some women from our group of his followers*
were at his tomb early this morning, and they came
back with an amazing report.

23 *They said his body was missing, and they had seen*
angels who told them Jesus is alive!

24 *Some of our men ran out to see, and sure enough, his*
body was gone, just as the women had said.'

25 *Then Jesus said to them, 'You foolish people! You find*
it so hard to believe all that the prophets wrote in the
Scriptures.

26 *Wasn't it clearly predicted that the Messiah would*
have to suffer all these things before entering his glory?'

27 *Then Jesus took them through the writings of*
Moses and all the prophets, explaining from all the
Scriptures the things concerning himself.

Luke 24:2–27

Haven't You Heard?

Mary, Wife of Clopas

Honestly, haven't you heard?

I was in deep disgust and disbelief.

Everyone, that is, *everyone*, was talking about
the outrageous and undignified death of Jesus
our nephew this weekend, which was to be our
celebrated Passover event. Just this morning, a
number of women, who were some of His close
followers, visited the tomb and claimed it was
empty — and yet how could that be?

Here was this *stranger* who knew nothing about
our culture, customs or ceremonies, asking about
things that seemed outside his normal realm.
Naturally, he didn't belong here, and I wasn't
about to start to give explanations about things
that hurt *so close to home*.

The stranger was insistent, asking, 'What were you discussing so intently?'

I rebuffed myself, refusing to answer. Through his own downcast face, my husband Cleopas saw through my annoyance, and decided to interject before I could say anything that might have come across as *inappropriate*. He responded with the very words that I was thinking.

'Sir, you must be the only person in Jerusalem who hasn't heard about all the things that have happened here the last few days.'

The stranger continued his enquiry, 'What things?'

Cleopas continued, battling the sadness that was flushing his eyes with tears.

'The things that happened to Jesus, the man from Nazareth. He was a prophet who did powerful miracles, and he was a mighty teacher in the eyes of G-d and all the people. But our leading priests and other religious leaders handed Him over to be condemned to death, and they crucified Him. We had hoped He was the Messiah who had come to rescue Israel. This all happened three days ago.'

He took a breath — the thought that their Hope, their Messiah, the Anointed One had perished

— this was all too much to reflect on, especially to the *uninitiated*.

'Then some women from our group of his followers were at His tomb early this morning, and they came back with an amazing report. They said His body was missing, and they had seen angels who told them Jesus is alive! Some of our men ran out to see, and sure enough, His body was gone, just as the women had said.'

His words trailed off, not expecting a reply. Confused and agitated, my husband needed time to breathe. This was a family matter, and we didn't feel right talking about it to outsiders.

We wanted to keep it within the family circle: Cleopas was the much younger brother to Joseph — Mary's betrothed husband. Together, we had helped to raise Jesus along with his other half-brothers after we had wed.

How could anyone else feel the pain we were in right now?

The stranger piped in, with a level of obstinate authority that jolted us to stop and listen.

'Why do you find it so hard to believe all that the prophets wrote in the scriptures? Wasn't it clearly predicted that the Messiah would have to suffer all these things before entering into His glory?'

We weren't ready for a history lecture. Nor ready to be called 'foolish' by an outsider. But there was no fight left in us to protest, and we were intrigued by what he might say next, so we continued to listen.

He walked us through the writings of Moses, then all the prophets, explaining all the things that were to happen to the Messiah. Example after example, scripture after scripture, he demonstrated that the Messiah was expected to be put to death, and what would happen as a result.

Our hearts burned intently; our sadness eased, and we wanted to hear more of this good news. The stranger put it all together like assembling a large puzzle that no-one had been able to piece together until now, as we moved closer to home.

It was late and he intended to continue on past our Emmaus home. Cleopas looked at me, our eyes danced for a second while we considered inviting him in for the night. This was no longer a stranger; this was someone we needed to listen to. Out of all the chaos, things were starting to make sense for once.

'Please sir, if you wouldn't mind, stay with us the night, as it is getting late.' Cleopas offered.

The invitation was accepted and we headed indoors to share a meal. The scene unfolded with a sense of familiarity, like a distant relative had returned home, as though we put on an old set of shoes that fit our feet snuggly.

'Shall we give thanks?' Excited, we nodded, as He blessed the meal, and we ate.

Suddenly, the room changed.
Our guest disappeared!
And our eyes opened.

Not that they were shut any, but we suddenly realised that *this was no stranger* that had beset us with questions on our trip home.

This was Jesus.

JESUS.

J - E - S - U - S

He had made an unexpected appearance. And we hadn't recognised Him.

Now, it all made sense.

No wonder our hearts burned within us as we walked on the road, as he explained the scriptures to us.

But how could this be? We saw Him die, saw where He was buried, and we couldn't believe the reports of the women that He could have been alive, despite the empty tomb.

And yet, the ancient stories *passed down from our fore-fathers* all seemed to point to this one Man in time, all saying the same thing about the One to come, who would be the Saviour of the world.

And we had missed it!

We quickly finished our meal, and decided that *although it was late*, there was no better time to tell the others of what just happened. Packing up, we headed back to Jerusalem.

This revelation was not simply a coincidence.

It was to lead to greater things.

Jesus was truly alive!

Via Lucis 6:

Jesus Breaks Bread

²⁸ *By this time they were nearing Emmaus and the end of their journey. Jesus acted as if he were going on,*

²⁹ *but they begged him, 'Stay the night with us, since it is getting late.' So he went home with them.*

³⁰ *As they sat down to eat, he took the bread and blessed it. Then he broke it and gave it to them.*

³¹ *Suddenly, their eyes were opened, and they recognized him. And at that moment he disappeared!*

³² *They said to each other, 'Didn't our hearts burn within us as he talked with us on the road and explained the Scriptures to us?'*

³³ *And within the hour they were on their way back to Jerusalem. There they found the eleven disciples and the others who had gathered with them,*

³⁴ *who said, 'The Lord has really risen! He appeared to Peter.'*

Luke 24:28–32

Our Hearts Were Burning

Cleopas, Brother of Joseph

'Stay the night with us, sir.' It was getting late, and we had travelled quite a distance from early in the day.

As children, our parents taught us that the way of kindness was to show hospitality to strangers and those less fortunate than ourselves. As a result, our family was close-knit, having taken in other family members to form a blended extended family. Together, we were eager to seek the will and the ways of the Lord Yahweh.

My mind raced back to the times of Jesus' childhood, and deep impressions swelled up inside me, the first of which was the extraordinary relationship between His parents.

Joseph, my *much older* brother, already with children, *though his wife had died*, was selected by the priests to wed Mary, the girl from the synagogue.

> Mary was the blessing that her parents had hoped and prayed for, but just as in times past her birth did not arrive in the normal way. Her mother Anne married Joachim, a devout Jew and a wealthy man. They had consecrated themselves to G-d, and settled in Nazareth, however like Sarai and Abram, they were childless as they were unable to conceive.
>
> The temple priests scolded Joachim as being sterile, so he retreated to the countryside to pray. During the 40 days that he was away, Anne grieved his absence and fervently promised G-d that, if given a child, she would dedicate it to the Lord's service.
>
> An angel appeared to both of them, announcing that Anne would conceive and bear a most wondrous child. The couple rejoiced at the birth of their daughter, whom Anne named Mary.
>
> When Mary was three years old, Joachim and Anne, in fulfillment of their promise, brought her to the Temple in Jerusalem, where they left her to be brought up by the priests. After

living in the temple for 10 years, she was of age to be married, so the priests assembled the eligible men of the line of David to determine who would become her husband, as was the custom to select a suitable partner from the woman's hometown, which in this case was Bethlehem.

And that's where my brother Joseph was introduced to her, as a single (yet widowed) man.

In those days the priests relied on a prophecy relating to the budding of Aaron's staff to determine who would be the one appointed to marry the girl. All the eligible young men brought their staff to the altar, laid it down and waited, hoping that they would be the one to win the temple girl; however for them the prophecy never came true.

Joseph, being older and with a family of his own, initially declined to attend, however at the insistence of the priests, conceded.

Finally, Joseph came and laid his staff on the altar — and it blossomed — just as did Levi's staff, which sprouted, budded and blossomed full with almonds to signify that the tribe of Levi was *the only rightful priestly leader amongst the tribes of Israel.*

In this manner the priests appointed Joseph to betroth the temple girl, accepting Mary to be his future wife, under the careful and watchful eyes of the priests — to the shock and disbelief of the younger men who had hoped to be her suitors.

The second memory of my brother reminded me that during their betrothal, Joseph was required to travel to his home town of Bethlehem — the town of David — to register for the first census taken by governor Quirinius of Syria, and he took his very pregnant fiancé with him.

Sadly, I must admit that our family could not accept them into our home. My family — Joseph's family — were indignant and outraged at the story of Mary's pregnancy, so we refused to take them in, and due to the census there was no room for them at the innkeepers residence.

Eventually the couple made a temporary home in a shelter of a rock face, at the family farm on the outskirts of town, which they shared for a time with various flocks and herds that gathered there for food and shelter.

And it was during that time that Mary, my sister-in-law-to-be, gave birth to a son, and was given the name Jesus.

I recall the time that we travelled down to
Jerusalem for the seven-day Passover festival.
We went as a family — Joseph, Mary, Jesus, as
well as myself (Cleopas), my wife Mary and my
boys James and Simeon. (These were cousins
to Jesus, but lived as a family since my wife had
passed away.) The boy Jesus was twelve years old,
and we performed our customary duties with
the sacrificial lamb to be eaten by the household
while in Jerusalem.

> The Passover meal was a celebration for the
> nation to recall the first-born male being spared
> from the angel of death that passed over the
> homes on the night that Israel fled Egypt.

> While at the Temple, Joseph and Mary
> presented Jesus to the temple leaders in
> order that He might be prepared for his bar
> mitzvah the following year. At the age of
> thirteen, all Jewish boys become responsible
> for their own actions, and they are recognised
> as full-fledged members of the Jewish
> community — granting them rights and
> responsibilities.

> It was, however, widely known that Jesus
> was not the son of Joseph through natural
> means, though we had grown to fully accept

Him into our family. The situation made it difficult for the priests to accept the candidate for this honourable celebration, as Joseph could not honestly declare the commemorative words, 'You are my beloved son, in whom I am well pleased.'

On the Sabbath after their thirteenth birthday, the boy is called up for the reading of a portion of the Torah section of the day — called an *aliyah*. This situation also meant that Jesus did not qualify to be called up for the reading of scripture.

Our family party departed and were a day on the journey towards Galilee when they noticed that Jesus was not in their company. Searching franticly, it took three days to eventually find him in the temple courts, sitting among the teachers — listening to them and asking them questions.

When His parents found Him, His mother said to Him, 'Son, why have you treated us like this? Your father and I have been anxiously searching for You.' The question seemed somewhat out of place, given the context, whereby Jesus knew the responsibility of His heavenly calling.

'Dear mother,' Jesus replied, 'didn't you know that I had to be in My Father's house?'

The incident left me a clear impression that the community would not allow Jesus to celebrate His coming of age next year, nor ever be accepted into normal Jewish society.

> At the age of thirty Jesus went to be baptised — it was his cousin John who was baptising people with a call to repentance at the Jordan River, five miles north of the dead sea. As Jesus came up out of the water, he saw heaven open and the Spirit of G-d descending on Him like a dove. A voice came from heaven, saying, 'You are My Son, whom I love; with You I am well pleased!'

> The Voice from heaven declared His coming of age! Although He could not have received the blessing from Joseph, Jesus was approved by His Heavenly Father in the sight of all those who were there with Him.

> Seven weeks later, Jesus returned from the desert where He had been fasting and had been tested by the Devil for forty days. He returned to our home town of Nazareth, and on the Sabbath day the scroll was handed to Him where He read from the prophet Isaiah,

> 'The Spirit of the Lord is upon me
> Because He has anointed me
> To proclaim good news to the poor.
>
> He has sent me to proclaim freedom
>   for the prisoners
> And recovery of sight for the blind,
> To set the oppressed free,
> To proclaim the year
>   of the Lord's favour.'

All the eyes of the people was fastened on Him, until He spoke, saying, 'Today this scripture is fulfilled in your hearing.'

Although Jesus missed out on reading the *aliyah* at the age of 13, there was no mistake that the scripture was His portion at this allocated time.

For me, these memories engrained within me and the other members of our close-knit family. We were there when the world rejected and despised Him, and we were there when Father G-d affirmed Him in the sight of all the people.

We had taken in Mary and Jesus as our own after my brother Joseph's death, but I did not realise that we were harbouring the Saviour of the World.

The breaking of bread with our Guest, whom
we had travelled with since Jerusalem, suddenly
took on new meaning and purpose. Although His
form was unrecognisable at the time, our hearts
burned, and suddenly it all made sense.

Via Lucis 7:

Jesus Appears in Jerusalem

35 *Then the two from Emmaus told their story of how Jesus had appeared to them as they were walking along the road, and how they had recognized him as he was breaking the bread.*

36 *And just as they were telling about it, Jesus himself was suddenly standing there among them. 'Peace be with you,' he said.*

37 *But the whole group was startled and frightened, thinking they were seeing a ghost!*

38 *'Why are you frightened?' he asked. 'Why are your hearts filled with doubt?*

39 *Look at my hands. Look at my feet. You can see that it's really me.*
Touch me and make sure that I am not a ghost, because ghosts don't have bodies, as you see that I do.'

40 *As he spoke, he showed them his hands and his feet.*

Luke 24:36–39

⸻Not a Ghost⸻

The Doubting and Frightened Disciples

Fear and disbelief gripped us, and we wrestled agonising thoughts — what was actually *real*, and what was *imaginary*?

The events of the last few days had freshly scarred our emotions: the hurried arrest, the illegal trial, the crucifixion, and the scattering where we ran for our own safety from those who might wish us harm. *If there were any followers of this Jesus, they should be captured and killed. We don't want an insurrection!* Such were the thoughts racing through our heads.

Our room was darkened to hide the few of us that had banded together through this time. We didn't need to be ratted out and handed over to the authorities; we were fighting for survival, at best.

What is going to become of us?
Have we followed Jesus all in vain?
What do we do now?
What can we believe any more?
Are these stories of a risen Jesus actually true?
Or are we hallucinating?
Nothing makes sense any more.
Surely, they have seen only a ghost!

Candles flickered, it was late, and a commotion
started from a knock at the door below.
Cautiously, the door was opened, and the
two from Bethany had returned back from
the Emmaus road with an exhausting yet
overwhelming story. Cleopas started:

'We were walking home when this man joined
us, who starting questioning what we were
talking about. We didn't know who it was at
the time, as God had kept his identity from
us, and we couldn't recognise him.'

'Along the way, we explained about Jesus —
who was a prophet that did powerful miracles,
and was a mighty teacher in the eyes of God
and all the people. We were surprised that
he was the only one in Jerusalem that hadn't
heard of these things, how the leading priests
and religious leaders had handed Him over to
be condemned to death, crucifying Him.'

We had hoped that He was to be the Messiah who had come to rescue Israel.

'Some women from our group had gone to the tomb this morning, and came back with a crazy report that the body of Jesus was missing and that an angel had appeared to them. Clearly, this all did not make sense to us, and we couldn't accept their report. What were they trying to achieve?'

'The man didn't seem too fussed with the story, and even went as far as to send us a rebuke — telling us from the Scriptures that it was predicted for the Messiah to suffer before entering into glory. He explained from Moses and the prophets how these events were to take place.'

'When we arrived near our place, we urged the man to come and stay with us, since it was late, his words had been burning in our hearts as he spoke — we wanted to hear more. When we broke bread for supper, he had given thanks, and suddenly — our eyes were opened and it all made sense.'

What made sense?

The cowering group had pressed in to hear the story, but were not quite convinced that what was said was true. They had faced many pressures over the last few days, and weren't thinking clearly enough to be able to evaluate yet another report from today.

The apostles and others that had gathered with them, listened intently to their story. Given that this was coming from Cleopas and Mary, this seemed credible — there could be some truth to this. Regardless, we wondered as to the real explanation and meaning of what was said. We reasoned that it could easily be explained by our knowledge of ghosts: those human spirits that were trapped between heaven and earth, who have not yet reached the place of the dead, or their heavenly home.

As we were talking, the room lit up.
In the centre, Jesus appeared.

'Peace, friends.'

Shaking and startled, we really were seeing a ghost before our eyes! We drew back against the walls, not knowing where to turn and escape this spiritual phenomenon.

Surely, this is the ghost of Jesus.
Has He come back to haunt us?
Did we fail Him so badly by not protecting Him
    from the authorities who killed Him?
What does He want with us now —
    to avenge His blood?

'Why are you frightened? Why are your hearts
filled with doubt?'

Can a ghost really speak to us?
Can't He see that we are scared because this
    doesn't occur to ordinary men and women?
We doubt that this is really a risen Messiah,
    there is only one resurrection that occurs after we die.

'Look at My hands and My feet. See! It is really Me!'

We observed — coming in close, cautiously.
But we dared not touch this figure, this apparition,
    not knowing what might happen next.

'Touch Me and make sure that I am not a ghost,
because ghosts don't have bodies, as you see that
I do.' And He showed us His hands and feet.

Not all of us had stayed for the crucifixion, except
Mary of Magdala, Mary of Cleopas (mother of
James and Joseph), Salome of Zebedee (mother of
James and John), the mother of Jesus and a few
others. The nail piercings from the cross were clearly

visible in His hands and feet, as had been explained
by these who were there.

Edging closer, He held out His hands, we stretched forward to see if this Ghost was real. Certainly, both hands and feet had substance, just as we had known Him earlier. Our confidence started to return; maybe our fears were not founded in fact?

'Do you have anything here to eat?' Jesus asked.

We went to the cupboard and took some fish from our rations, and watched as He ate it in front of our eyes. Just as described, the fish was warmly accepted and eaten by our Guest, demonstrating that ghosts don't eat, but humans do!

Certainly, this can't be a ghost!
Joy, wonder and amazement started to bubble up
from within us.
Are these reports from the women and Peter
and Cleopas actually true?
Is this the same Jesus, risen from the dead,
come to visit us?

Our caution turned to an excited whisper, growing to a clamber that turned our disbelief into excitement.

Surely, could this be the Christ?

'When I was with you before, I told you that
everything written about Me in the law of Moses and
the Prophets and in the Psalms must be fulfilled.'

> *Yes — you were with us, Lord.*
> *But we didn't understand that You had to go*
>   *through this.*
> *And now, NOW —*
> *WE CAN SEE!*
> *WE CAN SEE!*
> *Have we been so blind as to have missed this*
>   *all along?*
> *Something like scales have fallen from our eyes,*
>   *the blurry darkness has lifted.*
> *JESUS IS THE MESSIAH —*
> *THE PROMISED ONE.*

'Yes, it was written long ago that the Messiah
would suffer and die and rise from the dead on
the third day. It was also written that this message
would be proclaimed in the authority of his name
to all the nations, beginning in Jerusalem.'

> *Yes, Lord, now we see.*
> *The scriptures announced Your coming,*
>   *but we didn't look for it.*
> *We see your death fulfilled in the prophecies*
>   *of Moses, the Psalms and the Prophets.*
> *The sign of the prophet Jonah was that you would*
>   *rise on the third day, and that was all for us, too.*

'There is forgiveness for all who repent. You are witnesses of all these things.'

We have seen your death,
and now we have seen your resurrected body.
We know and believe that you are the Christ,
sent from heaven.
We can testify to what we have seen and heard,
but we feel so powerless and empty.
There is nothing in us that can boldly declare
what You want us to do.
We can tell Your story,
but who will believe our message?
Who will turn and repent to find this forgiveness
that You offer?
Lord, help us!

'And now I will send the Holy Spirit, just as My Father promised. But stay here in the city until the Holy Spirit comes and fills you with power from heaven.'

Stay and wait?
Yes, we can wait.
We know and believe that you are the risen Lord,
the promised Messiah.
And now we hear Your call to wait in the city,
here in the capital.

What is this Holy Spirit?
What is this power from heaven?
We don't yet know what it is,
   but since You have called us, we will wait and see.

Via Lúcis 8:

Jesus Gives Power to Forgive

²² *Then he breathed on them and said,*
'Receive the Holy Spirit.

²³ *If you forgive anyone's sins, they are forgiven. If you*
do not forgive them, they are not forgiven.'

John 20:22–23

⁓*Breath of Heaven*⁓

John, the Beloved

The candles flickered in the upstairs room where we had gathered, as we beheld this Presence in front of us.

The look on our faces revealed a mixture of emotions, detailing the depths of our heart — from the shock of experiencing a new reality of this unfolding story, to the overwhelming and surprising joy of this revelation.

A hush rolled over us like the quietening of an oceans roar as we grappled with the weight of it, the presence of heaven pierced the depths of our thoughts.

In this light nothing else mattered. All our ambitions, hopes and aspirations were pointless.

Our inner wrestlings and criticisms pecked at our soul; there really was no room for one-upmanship. Whoever was the least, or the greatest, amongst us, wasn't really a concern right now.

There was only one real point to this gathering, and that was the presence of Jesus amongst us.

Our eyes locked together on Him, waiting for a signal; instinctively we moved in to form a huddle to hear what He was about to say.

'Friends, receive the Holy Spirit.'

And with that, He blew on each of us. Suddenly the earthly weight that we carried was lifted, and we felt light on the inside. Whatever was holding us down had been rolled away, just like the stone that covered the entrance to the grave this morning.

It's as if … it's as if we were freed from a prison cell, and were seeing light of day once again! The words of the parable came back to us.

> Peter had asked, 'Lord how many times should I forgive the brother who sins against me — up to seven times?'
>
> Jesus answered, 'I tell you not seven times, but seventy times seven. The kingdom of

heaven is like a king who wanted to settle accounts with his servants.

A man was brought in who owed ten thousand bags of gold — much more than he was able to pay. The master ordered that he, his wife and children, and all that he had were to be sold to repay the debt.

The servant begged, 'Please master, be patient with me and I will pay back everything.'

The master of the servant took pity on him, cancelled the debt, and let him go.

When he had been set free, he found a fellow servant who owed just a hundred silver coins. The servant demanded of him, 'Pay back what you owe me.' And he began to choke him.

The fellow servant fell to his knees and begged for time, but mercilessly he was thrown into prison until he could pay the debt.

Other servants had witnessed these events and reported it to their master.

The master called in the servant, saying, 'You wicked servant, I had cancelled all that debt of yours because you begged me. Shouldn't you have had mercy on your fellow servant just as I had on you?'

In his anger, the master handed him over to be tortured until he should pay back all that he owed.

'This is how My heavenly Father will treat each of you unless you forgive your brother or sister from your heart.'

Yes, *we were free*, and any penalty or charge held against us had been lifted. This breath of heaven was refreshing, liberating, cleansing.

Drawing in, Jesus had more for us.

'Friends, if you forgive anyone's sins, they are forgiven. If you do not forgive them, they are not forgiven.'

The puzzle was starting to make sense. Inasmuch as we had experienced forgiveness, we were also given the task to forgive others. We were not only servants who had received a life-giving act of mercy from the Master; we had each been called to release the power of the Masters' forgiveness to others!

This paradox questioned our role as servants — *who has authority on earth to forgive sins?*

A flashback to the paralysed man boosted our confidence.

On a particular day, Jesus and His disciples
had come to His home town and a paralysed
man was brought to him lying on a mat.

When Jesus saw the faith of the men who
brought him, He said to the paralysed man,
'Son, take heart. Your sins are forgiven.'

Now there were some teachers of the law
watching on, and when they heard Him say
this, they said to themselves, 'This fellow is
blaspheming! Who can forgive sins but G-d
alone?'

Turning to them, Jesus said, 'Why are you
entertaining evil thoughts in your hearts?
Which is easier to say: 'Your sins are forgiven'
or 'Get up and walk'?

Let me demonstrate to you that the Son of
Man has authority on earth to forgive sins.'

So He turned to the paralysed man and said,
'Get up. Take your mat, and go home.'

Instantly the man rose to his feet, got up and
went home.

Clearly, the healing could not be discounted.
And for that matter, neither could the power of
forgiveness.

To move forward in the power of the kingdom of heaven, we need to become both the servant who receives forgiveness and the master who extends forgiveness to others.

This is the breath of heaven.

\

Via Lucis

Via Lucis 9:

Jesus and Thomas

24 *One of the twelve disciples, Thomas (nicknamed the Twin), was not with the others when Jesus came.*

25 *They told him, 'We have seen the Lord!'*

But he replied, 'I won't believe it unless I see the nail wounds in his hands, put my fingers into them, and place my hand into the wound in his side.'

26 *Eight days later the disciples were together again, and this time Thomas was with them.*
The doors were locked; but suddenly, as before, Jesus was standing among them. 'Peace be with you,' he said.

27 *Then he said to Thomas, 'Put your finger here, and look at my hands. Put your hand into the wound in my side. Don't be faithless any longer. Believe!'*

28   *'My Lord and my God!' Thomas exclaimed.*

29   *Then Jesus told him, 'You believe because you have seen
      me. Blessed are those who believe without seeing me.'*

John 20:24–29

See to Believe

Thomas, the Twin

I was expecting things to be different. For three years we had travelled with the Master, staying by His side as His 'disciples', or trained ones. We had given up every earthly thing to learn directly from our Rabbi the discipline required to become worthy of being called His followers.

Peter, James and John (the fishermen in the inner circle) had given up their livelihood to follow Jesus; I had left my home and business; others had stopped the clock on what they were doing to devote themselves entirely to this Man, and His teaching.

This was not just a fleeting moment for a weekend event, this was a complete change in lifestyle and productivity. We were being *interrupted*.

I was close to Jesus — though not in the inner circle — watching, listening and observing to learn how things fit together. For instance, how do you balance the obvious outward miracles, that brought favour and attention from the crowds, *with the religious elite* that snubbed and hated Him and wanted Him dead?

So, despite my position, I was cautious about the whole thing. Was this just a charade, or was there something greater at hand?

Just weeks ago, in the face of much opposition from the rulers, we headed to a small village outside Jerusalem, Bethany, where the brother of Mary and Martha had died. There really was no discussion about this, we were told by the Master, 'Lazarus is dead, and I am glad for your sakes that I was not there, that you may believe. Nevertheless, let us go to him.'

> *But Master, don't you know that they want to kill you?*
> *Don't you realise that you will put us all in danger*
>   *if we come with You?*
> *Don't you care for us, and our safety?*

I eyed the other disciples, hoping for their support — *were we really going to follow Jesus and risk our lives at this time?* But I got none.

Fine, if we are doing this, *then we are in it together.*

Turning to the group, I announced, 'Let us go
also, *that we may die with Him.'* My statement
was not intended to be prophetic, but rather a
pathetic attempt to sway everyone against this
decision. Hardly something that I could achieve
from within the group, and we went anyway.

The thought of this weighed heavily on my heart.
Was I really prepared to die for my Rabbi?

I was in two minds: the commitment to be
His disciple warred against my sense of self-
preservation and the desire to flee from tragedy at
any moment.

This feeling prised my heart open at the Supper,
when the Master was sharing His desire for us to
follow after Him, describing events and situations
about His Fathers' house, a place that sounded a
long way off at some distant point in the future.

Jesus shared, 'I go to prepare a place for you all.
There is more than enough room in My Father's
home. When everything is ready, I will come and
get you, so that you will always be with Me where
I am.'

Then He added, 'And *you know* the way to where I
am going.'

A silent pause fell across the room, as the depth of Jesus' gaze penetrated our souls, following on from what He said. *Did everyone truly understand what He was saying? Was Jesus sure that we knew what He was talking about?*

If it was about life on earth then He could have been more clear; if it was the after-life, then I'm not sure that we understood what He was saying.

> *What was 'My Fathers house'?*
> *When will everything be ready?*

I wanted more information, more clarity about this, and I wasn't the only one. So I asked, 'But Lord, we really don't know where you are going, so how can we know the way?'

Prodigiously, Jesus responded, 'Thomas. Friends.' He made sure we had His full attention.

'I am the Way. I am the Truth. I am the Life. No-one comes to the Father except through Me.'

This concept tore at my seams.

It didn't really answer my question, my burning desire
  to get to the heart of the matter.
We still didn't know what He meant,
  and what He intended.
This will have to be resolved later.

Jesus continued, 'If you had really known Me, you would know who my Father is as well. From now on, you do know Him and have seen Him.'

I wish this was clearer. But it wasn't.
We already had known Jesus, and had been with Him
  for three years now, and yet we hadn't encountered
  the Father.
This was all still a puzzle — and it frustrated me.

That's why tonight was a different occasion.

Tonight, I had returned to the Ten who had gathered in that upstairs room, who were meeting secretly away from the crowds and Jerusalem's leading rulers. For the last eight days I needed my own space, I needed time to think, to make sense of the experiences and teachings that we had together with our Rabbi.

None of this was clear to me — this whole *resurrection story* sounded like tales from madmen and crazy women that simply *wanted things to be so much different to what they appeared*. I was afraid that they had lost connection with reality, and were living a fantasy. It was starting to look very much like a hoax.

Before I had left, I'd made it *quite clear* that unless I see the nail prints in His hands and put my finger in His side, then I would *simply not believe*. There was no way that I could face the risk of persecution or death unless I had *substantial proof*—and this is something that they could not conjure up. It's the only way I could believe that what they were saying was true.

Tonight, *the unexpected* happened. We had locked the doors for fear that our gathering might be thrust apart by others with more sinister motives. I had come to this prayer meeting by invitation, though still not fully convinced that anything good was going to happen. Despite my own disbelief, the central Character appeared in the room amongst us.

'Peace be with you,' He said.

There was no doubt as to Who this was.

Approaching me, His broad smile brought peace that overcame the wrestling in my heart.

'Thomas, put your finger here, and look at My hands.' I reached out and grasped the hands of Jesus, felt the holes from the nails that had wrenched His flesh apart from the savagery of the cross. There were no doubts left in my mind, and I wasn't hallucinating. This truth was evident and lined up with what the others were saying.

'Now, put your hand into the wound in my side.'
This invitation made me uncomfortable, and
I had to draw in closer to the Lord to feel the
glorious wound. It was surely as everyone had
said, though I had not the courage to believe.

'Thomas, don't be without faith any longer. *Believe!*'

At this I fell to the floor, grasping His feet and
cried, 'Yes Lord, I believe! You are my Lord and
my G-d!'

'You believe because you have seen Me. Happy
are those who believe without seeing Me.'

Truly, my heart is now *settled*. My raging indecision
now *quashed*.

But not just as a *believer*, I will follow You all my days.

My Lord and my G-d.

Via Lucis 10:

Jesus and Peter

15 *After breakfast Jesus asked Simon Peter,*
    'Simon son of John, do you love me more than these?'
    'Yes, Lord,' Peter replied, 'you know I love you.'
    'Then feed my lambs,' Jesus told him.

16 *Jesus repeated the question: 'Simon son of John, do*
    you love me?'
    'Yes, Lord,' Peter said, 'you know I love you.'
    'Then take care of my sheep,' Jesus said.

17 *A third time he asked him, 'Simon son of John, do*
    you love me?'
    Peter was hurt that Jesus asked the question a third time.
    He said, 'Lord, you know everything. You know that
    I love you.'

    Jesus said, 'Then feed my sheep.

John 21:15–17

⟋Restored⟍

Simon Peter, the Failed Fisherman

It was early. We had been out all night and caught nothing. And I was done with waiting.

The sea was pleasant, the moon was right, and I desperately needed to escape the tormenting thoughts that plagued me since the arrest. This was my me time to recover, to get away, and forget the stupid promises that I could not keep.

Inside, I was hurting.

The Lord had predicted this, though I had vowed to be the key to His deliverance.

Even if everyone else denies You, I won't.

That was a promise that I was prepared to die for. And yet, just a few hours later, I had to save my own skin as the events turned against me.

I was a liar. And *I couldn't help myself,* let alone the Lord.

My gut needed to settle. I hadn't slept in days, and my mind continued to race through these events. I just needed to find my old life, find myself again with the tools that I grew up with, and *feel like me again.* Hence the boat trip.

The sun had cracked the horizon, and a gentle breeze stirred the water on the side of the boat.

At least I had support from a few friends that had also gone through the ordeal — Thomas, Nathanael, James, John and others. Although I couldn't look them in the eyes, I knew they were holding out for me. That's what mates are for. They were giving me time to find myself, and I sensed they were watching me closely to ensure that I didn't do anything rash to harm myself.

Indeed, I wasn't.

We saw a fire on the shore, and someone cooking. The smell of fresh fish caught our attention, blowing our way.

'Friends,' called the figure. 'Have you caught any fish?'

'No,' we replied. We felt envious that someone had their catch and had started to eat, while we had been out all night and were going to lose out on breakfast.

He responded, 'Throw your net out on the right-side of the boat and you'll get some!'

Well, it sounded like a crazy idea, but we had nothing to lose. We were sceptical but happy to take directions from someone who already caught his lot *and was having breakfast* — so we threw the nets over the other side of the boat.

Whoa.

WHOA.

'HELP!'

The nets strained under the weight, but did not break. We hauled the catch aboard — 153 large fish — *how could we have missed them, we were out all night?*

John tapped my shoulder and motioned, 'It's the Lord!'

Come again? Seriously, what is happening?

My soul awakened in a sea of desperate panic.

But it made sense.

His words echoed within me, just as they did in the beginning, here on the lake. 'Come, follow Me, and I will make you fishers of men.' At that point we had resolved to follow Him wherever He goes, and we had left our nets with our fathers, giving up the family trade, to be with the Lord.

And now, here we were back again, amidst the sea spray, the mist and the nets — we couldn't help feeling a sense of déjà vu.

We made it to the shore and tentatively, we ate the prepared fish. No-one dared speak, for we knew it was the Lord.

Just like He had appeared to the two from Emmaus, and again to those of us in the upper room, this was the third time that Jesus had appeared to us after He rose from the dead.

My guilt returned to haunt me.

How could I stand in His presence, having denied and run away from Him at a most crucial time? *I can never live this down.*

We'd just finished eating, the fish and warm bread from the fire were delicious, and I was planning my escape path. I really couldn't stand to be here much longer, the mere presence of the Lord was crushing me, and I felt burdened.

Then He caught my attention.

His soft eyes beckoned me over, 'Let's go for a walk.' We headed up the shore away from the others.

'Simon, son of John, do you love Me more than these?'

I looked down, tears started to fill my eyes but I wasn't going to let them break the surface; the question rolled around my mind, and confronted my act of desertion. 'Do you love Me more than these?'

Of course I love you Lord, but *'more than these'*? I had vowed to stand by You even if everyone else deserted You. You know that I would lay down my life sacrificially for You.

That is, *love You sacrificially.*

The question was now tearing up my ambitions, challenging my very core. How could I have denied Him and run away? How could I answer and say that I was prepared to lay down my life for Him *more than the others?*

I was trapped by my own promises and declarations. And He knew that there was no way I had fulfilled them.

'Yes, Lord, You know that I love You.'

My answer was feeble and weak. It spoke nothing of sacrificial love, only of friendship. I wasn't prepared to make any further bold declarations or promises that I knew I couldn't keep. *There were others that showed their love for Him more than me.* I felt so unworthy.

Looking towards me, the Lord wanted to reassure me. 'Feed my lambs.'

Immediately, I understood what He meant about the lambs. The lambs were His little ones, those whom He cared for with deep empathy, and who needed to be handled delicately. They needed a strong and caring leader, but someone who was not irrational, and someone who could relate to their weakness.

Walking further up the shore, He asked me again, 'Simon son of John, do you love Me?'

I was caught off guard with the repeated question, however this time there was no opportunity to show my loyalty by comparing with the others. *Do you love me sacrificially?* That is, *Would you lay down your life for Me?*

I recalled the final hours with Him in the upper room, before the arrest, before the unholy execution. The Lord had shared that to demonstrate the *greatest love* for others is to lay down your life for your friends. It was on that dark night, when we needed to stay by Him, that we all fled — while He laid down His life for us.

Again, I couldn't honestly respond to the question. I couldn't find it in me to say that I would lay down my life for Him. Inside I was frail, and my weakness held me back. I loved Him, but I wasn't prepared to make any more irrational vows about my how far that connection would go.

'Lord,' I winced, 'You know I love You *as a friend.'*

I felt bad having to admit my level of limited capability, when clearly He was asking for more than mere friendship.

'Then feed My lambs.'

Oh, that I could only do that! At this point, I could hardly feed myself, let alone others. I was emotionally drained, and the thought of feeding and caring for others was stretching the limits of my commitment. I let it rest in my mind, and accepted the call. A sense of peace came from the restoration that was happening between us.

We travelled a little further down the shore, and finally stopped. The sun was high, and the breeze stirred my hair.

Resting His arm on my shoulder, grabbing my full attention, Jesus asked, 'Simon, son of John, do you love Me as a friend? Do you have affection for Me?'

This time the Master's question had been downgraded — not calling me to compete with others; not calling to lay my life down for Him. He was simply asking me if I had affection for Him, if I loved Him as a friend.

And this hurt.

I didn't realise it; I had always reckoned Jesus as my friend. Though He was the one who called us His friends. But on that fateful night I had run away to desert Him, cursed myself, and claimed that I had never known Him.

What sort of friend does that?

The question pierced deep into the core of my being, challenging who I was and what I stood for in life. How could I demonstrate being a friend to anyone, when I was prepared to throw away our relationship in order to save my own skin?

The grief from this was unbearable.

'Lord, You know all things. You know that I love You as a friend.'

Inside I started to weep. I couldn't believe that I would be confronted for my loyalty, my self-sacrifice, and now my friendship.

He held me there for some time. There was nothing else to say, really, just an embrace.

We stood together in silence for some time; the weight of the world lifted. Waves of pure golden love enveloped me, and the sense of His Heavenly Presence overwhelmed me. This restoration was like nothing that I had experienced before. I felt alive again. Freed.

'Feed My sheep.' This final affirmation was the call to ministry, but not in worldly governance. It was a call to friendliness, being prepared to walk with the lowly and those who were not-so-privileged.

Finally, I no longer needed to flee. I was home.

Via Lucis 11:
Jesus Sends the Disciples

¹⁶ _Then the eleven disciples left for Galilee, going to the mountain where Jesus had told them to go._

¹⁷ _When they saw him, they worshiped him—but some of them doubted!_

¹⁸ _Jesus came and told his disciples, 'I have been given all authority in heaven and on earth._

¹⁹ _Therefore, go and make disciples of all the nations, baptizing them in the name of the Father and the Son and the Holy Spirit._

²⁰ _Teach these new disciples to obey all the commands I have given you. And be sure of this: I am with you always, even to the end of the age.'_

Matthew 28:16–20

⌁Sent⌁

Andrew, Simon Peter's Brother

It started when we were drawn to the Jordan River, to see a man wearing camel skins and a leather belt around his waist. We had heard that his only foods were locusts and wild honey, and his message was strong and direct.

> John *the Baptiser* had created a stir in all Jerusalem, with many people streaming from there and all Judea to come to the Jordan Valley, north of the town.

> 'Turn from your sins and prove it by your actions!' he declared. And when they had confessed what they had been doing wrong against G-d and man, he accepted them to be baptised as a demonstration of their confession.

One by one I watched the stream of people come to be baptised at the Jordan River, and was also drawn by some mysterious force to join the activity, make my own confession, and be baptised.

And then there was Jesus.

He had come to the Jordan to partake of this activity, and although he had nothing to declare, John accepted him to be baptised.

As Jesus went into the water and was drawn up again, the heavens opened and a dove descended on Him. A booming voice came from the heavens saying, 'This is My dearly loved Son, who brings Me great joy.'

The next day, I heard the Baptiser declare, 'Look! The Lamb of G-d who takes away the sins of the world!'

My excitement bubbled over at this, so I left John and ran to my brother Simon, to bring him to *the Messiah*.

This is *the One* that our parents and forefathers had told us about. This prophet was legendary in Israel before He became flesh and dwelt amongst us. Since I was a young child, we had been eager to find this promised Saviour.

Upon arrival, Jesus looked intently at him and said, 'Your name is Simon, son of John — but you will be called Cephas or Peter,' which means *a stone or a piece of rock*.

From this time we wanted to follow Jesus.

He left the next day for the region of Galilee, home of many famous Rabbis, where their students, called *disciples*, would be taught the scriptures and their application to daily living. The Rabbi would select and call disciples; a student could not simply claim to be of a certain teacher.

Not having been called, we returned to our family business — we were fishermen in the area of Galilee. One day while we were throwing our nets into the water, Jesus called out to us. 'Come follow Me, and I will show you how to fish for people!'

This was the prompting that we had been waiting for. Simon and I rolled up the nets into our boat and anchored it to the shore. We said goodbye to our families, and left to follow the Rabbi. Further up the shore Jesus

called out to our other friends, James and
John, and they too left their family business
in the hands of their father and hired hands,
and came to follow Him.

That's how it all came about, but *tonight* was different.

Tonight, we were led up a mountain near
Bethany, the Mount of Olives, where Jesus often
prayed — and where He spent His last night on
earth near the rock of anguish, and where an
angel appeared to give Him strength through
His sufferings and death.

Tonight, we were saying more goodbyes. The
Eleven sat in a circle around the rock, and waited
for the Master to appear. He had told us not to
be concerned about the times or dates that the
Father had set for events on the earth and with
Israel. *His business was much greater than what we could
imagine, and we were concerned with too much here.*

Suddenly appearing among us, He left us with this
message. 'Soon I will send the Holy Spirit to you,
just as My Father promised. But stay here in the
city until the Holy Spirit comes and fills you with
power from heaven. For you will receive power
when the Holy Spirit comes upon you. And you
will be My witnesses, telling people about Me

everywhere — in Jerusalem, throughout Judea, in Samaria, and to the ends of the earth.'

Then lifting His hands to heaven, He pronounced a priestly blessing over us. 'I have been given all authority in heaven and on earth. Therefore, go and make disciples of all the nations, baptizing them in the name of the Father and the Son and the Holy Spirit. Teach these new disciples to obey all the commands I have given you. And be sure of this: I am with you always, even to the end of the age.'

While we were worshipping Him, Jesus was taken up into heaven until a cloud hid Him from our sight. As we were looking for Him, two men in dazzling white robes stood with us. 'You Galileans, why are you standing here staring into heaven? Jesus has been taken from you into heaven, but someday He will return from heaven in the same way you saw him go!'

Our lives and our purpose, had changed significantly, *drastically*, from the time we were called to follow Him, and to 'catch men' instead of fish, until now, where we were now called to make disciples *just as Jesus had made us His disciples.*

The command was a stipulation and an ultimatum.

Go and make disciples.

Via Lucis 12:

Jesus Ascends to Heaven

⁹ *After saying this, he was taken up into a cloud while they were watching, and they could no longer see him.*

¹⁰ *As they strained to see him rising into heaven, two white-robed men suddenly stood among them.*

¹¹ *'Men of Galilee,' they said, 'why are you standing here staring into heaven?*
Jesus has been taken from you into heaven, but someday he will return from heaven in the same way you saw him go!'

Acts 1:9–11

⸌Why Are You Staring?⸍

Two White-Robed Men, the Ascension

We could never have imagined today's events.

For the last forty days, after the resurrection, we continued to have encounters with Jesus. Sometimes He would share a meal with us, and at other times He wanted to provide us with convincing proofs that He was *truly alive* and not simply a figment of our imagination.

During this period He spoke about the kingdom of G-d — how He was setting it up, what He had done in order to become the Ruler of the Kingdom of Heaven, and how heaven works in relation to the earth.

If we ever felt that things were unfinished, it was because we started to understand that He was shortly going to leave us and permanently return to heaven.

And that made us uneasy, to say the least.

Not that we feared His departure, but we felt quite alone with the thought that our Leader was no longer going to be with us *on location*. We recalled the words that He spoke to us prior to His death.

'You are filled with grief because I have
    said these things.
Truly, truly I tell you, it is for your good
    that I am going away.
Unless I go away the Advocate will not come
    to you; but if I go, I will send him to you.'

The Advocate, the Comforter, was to be sent to us, *but only if He was to go away.*

Our hearts raced, looking for answers, but the only conviction that we shared was that Jesus meant what He said — once He leaves, He will send us the Comforter to be with us forever. These sound thoughts resonated with us, calming our grief.

During a meal, Jesus gave us this command.

'Do not leave Jerusalem.
Wait for the gift that my Father has promised,
    which you heard Me speak about.
For John baptised in water, but in a few days
    you will be baptised in the Holy Spirit.'

We took little comfort from His words, despite how reassuring they were intended to be. But having seen and heard the miracles, signs and wonders of the kingdom of G-d over the last forty days, we had enough evidence and proof that a new beginning was about to unfold.

So we decided to continue together in the city, and wait for the promise to come.

After the meal, we headed to the Mount of Olives, not too far from Bethany. Again, Jesus reassured us.

'I am going to send you what My Father has promised.

But stay here in the city until you have been clothed with power from on high.'

And with that, He lifted up His hands and blessed us. Streams of sadness filled our eyes as we bid Him goodbye one last time, until at last a cloud hid Him from sight as He entered heaven.

This was solemn time; heart-breaking with both hope and sadness, a time that we will remember for years to come — and especially so if He didn't hold fast to His word!

While we were gazing into the sky, *two men in dazzling white clothes* appeared beside us. It was quite evident that they were not from this place. Their clothes were awash with the glory of heaven, brilliant white like the raiment of angels. Apparently they had been there the whole time.

Peter, James and John had mentioned the time that Moses and Elijah joined Jesus on Mount Transfiguration, discussing the events that were soon to take place in Jerusalem that would lead to Jesus' death and resurrection. They recalled the *dazzling white* clothes filled with the glory of heaven, until a cloud covered them on the hill that day.

Similarly, we remembered the women's stories from the tomb, early on the Sunday morning — Mary Magdalene, Mary the mother of James and several other women — and how the *two men in dazzling robes* suddenly appeared to them.

'Why are you looking for the living among the dead? He isn't here — He is risen from the dead! Remember what He told you back in Galilee.'

These two men were not unfamiliar with the life of Jesus, and they were not simply casual observers or passers-by. They had been part of *the testimony of Jesus* to record the events of His life on earth in the books of heaven.

They were present on the mountain to confirm the events that were to take place concerning His death; they appeared at the tomb to witness His resurrection; and now on this high mountain they stood to provide a witness to His ascension.

'Men of Galilee, why do you stand here looking into the sky? This same Jesus, who has been taken from you into heaven, will come back in the same way you have seen him go into heaven.'

The Eleven strained through their sadness at the departure of Jesus, faced with this challenge by the two witnesses.

'Why do you stare, as though He is never coming back?'

Via Lucis 13:
Waiting for Jesus

¹² *Then the apostles returned to Jerusalem from the Mount of Olives, a distance of half a mile.*

¹³ *When they arrived, they went to the upstairs room of the house where they were staying.*

Here are the names of those who were present: Peter, John, James, Andrew, Philip, Thomas, Bartholomew, Matthew, James (son of Alphaeus), Simon (the zealot), and Judas (son of James).

¹⁴ *They all met together and were constantly united in prayer, along with Mary the mother of Jesus, several other women, and the brothers of Jesus.*

Acts 1:12–14

⸺*Prayer Vigil*⸺

Mary, the Contemplator

It was a glorious moment for all of Israel to behold: Herod the Great had just rebuilt the Jerusalem Temple, and was being dedicated to YHWH in an official ceremony that lasted many weeks. People streamed to Jerusalem from both Judea and Israel with sincere gratitude in their hearts, to recommit their lives to the Lord, and take part in the official celebrations that the nation had missed for several hundred years, since the captivity.

Year after year, my parents Joachim and Anne came down from Nazareth, bringing their offerings and sacrifices, and with a special request — that, *even though they were past the age of childbearing,* they might find favour in this regard.

The temple priests held no pity for Joachim —
whose religious fervour should have produced
more than the evidence of material wealth, but
should have also found favour with G-d to
produce a family — and they scolded him for
his inability to produce a child that might be
useful for running the ordinances of this newly
completed Temple.

The priests' berating caused my father to run into
hiding in the nearby countryside, where he fasted
for forty days, and at the end of that time an angel
appeared to answer his prayers, and those of my
mother: they were to have a *most wondrous child.*

It wasn't long before they rejoiced at my birth,
and in response to their pledge they presented me
back to the priests three years later, when my time
to be weaned had been completed.

I was the temple's servant girl. My duty was to the
temple, to the priests, and to those who came to
offer sacrifices and offerings in religious ceremony.
And I was waiting for my destiny to be revealed.

One decade since my arrival, the priests felt the
need to find a suitable marriage partner for me,
and through a selection process I was betrothed
to Joseph, of the line of King David, from
Bethlehem. During our betrothal period I was

granted leave from the temple to spend time with my parents in Nazareth, who had continued to live in the Galilean village.

While I was there, I had an extraordinary encounter with an angel, who brought a *more extraordinary* message:

'Greetings, favoured woman! The Lord is with you!'

I wondered what sort of greeting this was.

'Don't be afraid, Mary, for you have found favour
     with G-d!
You will conceive and give birth to a son,
     and you will name Him Jesus.
He will be very great and will be called the
     Son of the Most High.
The Lord G-d will give Him the throne
     of His ancestor David.
And He will reign over Israel forever;
     His Kingdom will never end!'

I asked the angel, *'But how can this happen?
I am a virgin.'*

The angel replied:

'The Holy Spirit will come upon you, and the
     power of the Most High will overshadow you.
So the baby to be born will be holy, and He will
     be called the Son of God.

What's more, your relative Elizabeth has
  become pregnant in her old age!
People used to say she was barren, but she has
  conceived a son and is now in her sixth month.
For the word of God will never fail.'

'I am the Lord's servant. May everything you have
said about me come true.'

And then the angel left.

At this exciting news I packed and hurried to see
my *much older* cousin Elizabeth, travelling from
Nazareth to Hebron in the hill country of Judea,
some thirty miles south of Jerusalem.

I found things to be just as the angel said.

When I arrived, Elizabeth's child leaped within
her, and she was filled with the Holy Spirit.

Elizabeth gave a glad cry and exclaimed to Mary:

'God has blessed you above all women,
  and your child is blessed.
Why am I so honoured, that the mother of
  my Lord should visit me?
When I heard your greeting,
  the baby in my womb jumped for joy.
You are blessed because you believed
  that the Lord would do what he said.'

At her greeting, a song of praise bubbled up from within me.

'Oh, how my soul praises the Lord.
How my spirit rejoices in God my Saviour!
For He took notice of His lowly servant girl,
    and from now on all generations will call
    me blessed.
For the Mighty One is holy,
    and He has done great things for me.
He shows mercy from generation to generation
    to all who fear him.
His mighty arm has done tremendous things!
He has scattered the proud and haughty ones.
He has brought down princes from their thrones
    and exalted the humble.
He has filled the hungry with good things
    and sent the rich away with empty hands.
He has helped His servant Israel and remembered
    to be merciful.
For He made this promise to our ancestors,
    to Abraham and his children forever.'

I stayed with Elizabeth three more months,
until the birth of her child, *John*, and then left
for Nazareth to stay with my parents until
our scheduled marriage date. At this time the
evidence of my pregnancy was beginning to
show: *I was in my first trimester.*

I shared the angelic encounter with my family: that I was to bear *the Saviour of the world;* and of my time with Elizabeth, who gave birth *despite her old age.* My parents were overjoyed with the news, praising G-d for His goodness and mercy to Israel.

Together we wanted to know what the destiny of this Child that I was bearing would be.

During this period Governor Augustus decreed that a census should be taken throughout the Roman Empire. This required everyone to return to their ancestral towns to register, and since I was betrothed to Joseph I was required to travel back to Joseph's home town, Bethlehem. Joseph's family, however, were not as accepting of the miraculous vision and circumstances that led to me being somewhat pregnant, and while we were there I gave birth to my firstborn son, whom Joseph named *Jesus* at the command of the angel.

That night, a number of shepherds arrived with their lanterns and torches, leaving their sheep in the fields, in response to an angelic visitation.

'I bring you good news that will bring great joy
   to all people.
The Saviour — yes, the Messiah, the Lord —
   has been born today in Bethlehem,
   the city of David!

And you will recognize him by this sign:
  You will find a baby wrapped snugly
  in strips of cloth, lying in a manger.'

With this sign, and others, G-d demonstrated
to us that this child was of no ordinary origin,
verifying the words that the angel Gabriel had
spoken to me in the beginning.

I often contemplated the significance of this, and
how it would work its way out in my life.

Joseph and I visited Jerusalem every year for
Passover. When Jesus was twelve years old,
we attended the festival as usual and started
to return home to Nazareth. Not knowing
our son was absent, we searched frantically
among our family clans but could not find Him.
Returning to Jerusalem, we found Him sitting
with the religious teachers, listening to them and
asking questions. They were all amazed at His
understanding, and His answers.

We were hurt that Jesus had not let us know that
He was staying behind, and scolding Him I asked,
'Son, why have you done this to us?'

Jesus responded, 'But why did you need to
search? Did you not know that I must be in My
Father's house?'

Confused, Joseph and I contemplated what he meant, because we did not understand at the time. We returned to Nazareth where He was obedient to us, and watched as He grew in stature and favour with G-d and men.

Little did we know that the temple would be a place of solace for Jesus, too.

Over the years there are many, many stories that I've stored up in my heart about what Jesus said and did — I could write a book about them.

But this morning, here in this upper room, a fresh breeze filled the air. The seven weeks had dramatically changed everyone's lives, and we had now gathered in one place to pray as a newfound community of Jesus-believers.

We had been told to wait in Jerusalem *until we were filled with power from on high*, and it was in this spacious room that 120 of us were meeting each day to pray, with the expectation that something significant was to take place.

We were waiting for destiny to be fulfilled.

Each day we took turns to share our own personal stories of how Jesus had impacted our lives. From the fishermen to the tax collectors, each one shared their own meaning and perspective, creating a mosaic narrative that helped grow everyone's appreciation of what G-d was doing amongst His people.

From being a lowly servant girl, to now watching over the spiritual house that was being built amongst us, the temple has always been a place of refreshing for me.

It's my waiting place.

Via Lucis 14:
Jesus Sends the Holy Spirit

2   *Suddenly, there was a sound from heaven like the roaring of a mighty windstorm, and it filled the house where they were sitting.*

3   *Then, what looked like flames or tongues of fire appeared and settled on each of them.*

4   *And everyone present was filled with the Holy Spirit and began speaking in other languages, as the Holy Spirit gave them this ability.*

Acts 2:2–4

⸺ *The Flame* ⸺

Peter, the Bold

I was with 120 other Jesus-believers in the upper room, waiting, just as we were told to do; and we were praying, eating and sharing life together. It had been 7 weeks since the Passover, which resulted in the Crucifixion of Jesus. Then on Sunday morning there were angels at the tomb that announced the Resurrection. Later that day Jesus appeared to Mary Magdalene, Cleopas and his wife, and later that evening, the Eleven.

These post-resurrection encounters were obvious, and we had been instructed to gather in Jerusalem and wait for what was to come. We continued to meet and lodge in the upstairs room, where the disciples had gathered for the Last Supper on that fateful night. As we met, we eagerly sought to know what was coming next.

What would it be?
When would it happen?
Was this going to be a personal revelation
  of the Lord?

Together we wanted to know more; *we didn't want to miss a thing.*

We searched through the scriptures, researching what the prophets had spoken about the life, death and resurrection of Jesus. These last seven weeks were filled with daily sharing of the historic texts from the Patriarchs, Psalms and Prophets.

And today was Pentecost.
In our language, *Shavuot*.

This is the day we celebrated the giving of the Torah to Moses on Mount Sinai, and is one of the three pilgrim festivals that take us back to the Holy Temple in Jerusalem each year. Steeped in austere tradition, we present the first fruits of our harvest to G-d at the Tabernacle, carrying it on our shoulders, arriving in music and song. Here we would bring a sample of the good things from the *land that was flowing with milk and honey.*

It was an annual experience that united us, bringing the foreigners home in a way to broadcast thankfulness to the Holy One of Israel.

And this year was no exception, with many of
our kinsmen returning to the Temple bringing
their gifts. The town was jostling with excitement
as we were continually reminded of the good
things that G-d had provided us.

We met together, the upper room filled with
joyous music, expressing our thanks to G-d for
everything that had been revealed to us about
Jesus. And we were waiting for the fulfilment of
the Promise.

Suddenly, the room filled with the blowing of
a violent wind. The doors and windows shook
and shuddered, an extraordinary spiritual
manifestation halted our prayers and readings
and singing, and the room was filled with a holy
physical presence of heaven.

Eyes locked towards one another around the
room, no-one missed this; we were all caught up
in the breaking revelation of heaven's outpouring
to earth. This was no mistake, there was now *no
room for disbelief* — this wasn't some magic trick
conjured up by the leaders.

The wind swirled and danced around us for
what seemed like minutes, then suddenly broke
into flames like fire and came to rest on each of
us. The flames rested on our heads, the feeling

of warmth spread from the top of our head and drenched us like a warm blanket down our shoulders and through to our feet. We were completely overcome with the beautiful sweet feeling of heavenly peace, and our hearts filled with joy.

Our *Shavuot,* the first fruits of the harvest was being fulfilled *in a heavenly sense!* Jesus had entered the room to accept His first fruits, the 120 that had faithfully come together and celebrate this time. This was 'the power from on high' that was mentioned when He ascended, saying, *'Behold I send you the Promise of the Father upon you; moreover remain in the city until you be clothed with power from on high.'*

Certainly these flames wrapped around us like new clothes, not that we were being burned as it was not an earthly flame. Our human efforts and strength sapped away in comparison to what was a new dynamic, a heavenly power, that instantly brought confidence to our spirit. Everything that we had learned, practised and witnessed was merely *head-knowledge* but here in this room, *everything came to light* and gave us understanding and meaning.

We had come alive!

As the heavenly flames filled and engulfed us, the spiritual presence became heavier, the atmosphere was electric, and a Shekinah glory filled the room — reminding us of the times when Moses entered the Tent of Meeting.

The outpouring became strong to *overpowering*, and the heavenly flames broke upon in forms of praise, worship and prophecy.

Young men started *declaring* things that were being revealed to them in the spirit, right at that moment, to others near them.

Young women *unexpectedly* spoke of things to come, carried along by the Spirit, and explained depth and meaning of the scriptures about Jesus that they had learned by rote from youth.

Old men, laying on the ground in a state of deep sleep that had overcome them, shared *revealed dreams* and knowledge that only could have been provided from a revelation in heaven.

The day turned into a somewhat chaotic spiritual sensory explosion that had no earthly explanation, an experience that *no-one had heard or seen before.*

A crowd gathered; apparently we had become quite a spectacle, overflowing onto the streets from our upper room, onto the pavement, and into the city.

To most people we sounded like a mob of unruly drunkards! Each had their own experience, in whatever way the Spirit of G-d revealed things to them.

Amazed and perplexed, they asked, 'What does this mean?'

My spirit filled with revelation, scriptures from the prophet Joel jumped to mind, and I addressed the growing crowd to answer their questions.

'Fellow Jews, and everyone else living in Jerusalem,
  let me explain this to you — listen carefully
  to what I am about to say.
These people are not drunk, as you're suggesting.
It's only 9am, and no one drinks until later
  in the day!

But G-d tells us through the prophet Joel,

> 'In the last days
> I will pour out My Spirit on all people.
> Your sons and daughters will prophesy.
> Your young men will see visions.
> Your old men will dream dreams.
> Even on My servants, both men and women,
> I will pour out My Spirit in those days,
> And they will prophesy."

The people became silent.

Was this really the promise of the last days,
   as spoken by Joel?
It certainly didn't feel like a natural thing.
And yet, it all made sense.

This was the promise — *the fulfilment of the
promise* — that Jesus Christ had come to give
those who believe.

The flame was lit!

Concluding Thoughts

I would like to thank you for journeying together with me through 28 days of reflection and contemplation around the death and resurrection of Jesus, visiting the 14 Stations of the Cross and the 14 Stations of the Light.

At each of the Stations we have taken a 'behind the scenes' look at how events might have transpired for that person or group of people. We won't know for sure if the storyline correctly captures the complete set of events, as the written records do not include the full depth of history, but I hope that in no way that it has it been misleading or a misrepresentation of the written Word. In some cases, I've used poetic licence to help us engage more intimately at some Stations, and I pray that you grant me the grace to express my opinions in this way.

My aim has been to place you on location during these events, and if I've achieved that then my main mission has been accomplished. For the benefit of reflection and contemplation, the intent has been to stop at each Station, slow down and let the word speak to us.

Some of us may have been moved emotionally by the brutality of the soldiers during the crucifixion, or felt the healing and restoration during the discourse between Peter and Jesus, or shocked by the rapid rancid thoughts of Judas. Prayerfully, our souls have been touched in some way as a result of this encounter with Jesus. How will we move forward into the life that God has called us to?

Others may have found points of interest or debate in a re-interpretation of historical accounts, challenging what we have been taught or learnt. By including a lot of the back-story events in the Stations, we gain a broader picture of what might have motivated someone to act the way they did. There is likely to be a much larger story than what I've been able to capture in these few short pages, but I hope it is enough to stimulate further discussion and personal research so that we can grow into a broader sense of understanding.

And I am aware that there will be others that are ready to burn me at the stake as a heretic for suggesting that events might have happened in certain ways – ways which would oppose an established line of thinking or education. Given that there have been major religious wars over the centuries that fully support one opinion over another, I can't see that this will end here. No-one can know the full facts of history, and other than the Biblical quotes for the Stations I've deliberately excluded sources, references and a bibliography to avoid confrontation. For this reason it is published as Biblical fiction.

Finally, as we move past the Easter period, beyond the Ascension and enter the age of the Spirit-filled Church, I pray that our daily walk can reflect the power of Jesus within each of us.

May our lives demonstrate the life changing work of the Stations of the Cross in all repentance and humility, embracing the cross and laying down our own wishes or desires in love for others.

May the Holy Spirit grant us fullness of the Presence of G-d from our encounters at the Stations of the Light, so that we live powerful lives for Christ.

Thank you, Lord, for your presence with us this day.

As we depart from this space now, we ask you to bless us throughout the remainder of the day and guide us safely home.

About the Author

Brother Brad Smith is a Brisbane-born Aussie and grew up in a variety of church denominations in both the city and rural contexts. He has been working with OMF for many years on short term mission trips to Japan. He is married and has two adult children.

Brother Brad has a passion to express the message of the gospel in simple terms and holds a Diploma of Theology from Harvest Bible College, Australia. Brother Brad enjoys writing about theological topics, explaining Biblical subjects in simple terms.

www.brotherbrad.com

Other Books by
⌒Brother Brad Smith⌒

The Advent is a 24-day devotional that walks us through a Biblical calendar of prophecies and events in the lead up to Christmas Day.

Use each chapter of The Advent to enter into a time of reflection and spiritual growth in preparation for the most widely recognised day in the Christian calendar: the birth of Jesus Christ.

Brother Brad Smith brings together Biblical research, historical facts and other stories to present the promises given by God about the coming of Christ the Messiah to the nation of Israel. Follow the 'reason for the season' through the pages of the Old and New Testaments and uncover the prophetic promises that were spoken about Christ.

Challenge your spiritual growth in the chapters of The Advent in the 24 days leading up to Christmas Day.

Reflect on the daily readings to participate in the reason why Jesus came to earth, as promised to Eve in the garden of Eden, to Abraham, the prophets and to those surrounding His birth.

Step into the promises of history and become part of the storyline to experience the love of God in Christ Jesus.

Available online in ebook or paperback version from **www.brotherbrad.com**

She is highly praised and respected as the mother of Jesus Christ. But who would have known the level of grief that she was to go through when she accepted the calling from the angel Gabriel?

Traditionally identified as Mariam in scripture and translated simply as Mary, she is known by many other names by her devotees, such as the Virgin Mary, the Blessed Mother, Madonna, Mother of Mercy, God-bearer (Theotokos), The Holy Virgin and many others.

Mariam's Memoirs takes you on a journey through the account of her lifetime in this holy position where she recounts the stories at the end of her life so that they can be passed down to future generations. She is considered to be a primary source for the compilation of the gospels in the New Testament.

The prophecy of Simeon in the temple was a declaration of pain that accompanied her throughout her lifetime: *and a sword will pierce your very soul.* As her stories reveal, see how the sword affected her life and calling in ways that we would not have known.

Available online in ebook or paperback version from **www.brotherbrad.com**